The

Dreamer

His Dreamseekers

Book 1

By

Ronna M. Bacon

Mark 9:23 "Jesus said to him, "If you can believe, all things are possible to him who believes."
5

1 Corinthians 2:9 "Eye has not seen, nor ear heard, nor have entered into the heart of man the things which God has prepared for those who love Him."

NKJV

Table of Contents

Chapter 1

Shutting the hatch of his SUV, Evan Brant stood, his hand resting against the window. He was unsure of the steps that he was taking in his life. He raised his face to the warm summer sun and closed his eyes. *Please, Lord, guide me as to where I should go. I need to catch a break, to get some rest. I have dreams that I want to follow. You know what they are. I pray, dear Lord, that I can at least fulfill one. Which one? That's Your choice, Dear Lord.* He finally lowered his head, his eyes on the keys that he was rubbing between fingers.

Now where, Evan? He questioned where he should be heading. He was leaving the town of Elmton, where he had resided for a number of years, that much he knew. He sighed, walking around to open the driver's door and slip behind the wheel. He was footloose and fancy-free as the old saying went. Evan pulled away from the apartment building that he had called home for so many years. That is, when he wasn't working undercover as a police officer. The last case had drained him the most, he thought. He had approached his supervisor, a sergeant on the county force and tendered his resignation. The man had looked at him, shook his head, and questioned if Evan really knew what he was doing. He was the best one that they had for undercover work.

Evan had stared past him that day, his eyes on the window and watching the clouds scud through the sky before he had nodded.

"It is, Sarge. This last case? It did me in. I'm burnt out. It's been coming but losing that young child to the kidnappers? I can't do it anymore." Evan had finally lowered his eyes to see the compassion and understanding in the other man's eyes. "I have to. I'm not sure where I'll go or what I'll do but it's not here. Not anymore. With Mom and Dad gone, I have no links to this area anymore."

"You do, Evan. You have many friends who will miss you." The sergeant had risen to shake Evan's hand before he wished him well. He watched his young officer hesitate before he turned and walked away. *We'll miss you, Evan,* he murmured. *You are one of the best I have seen my whole career. You're burnt out, chewed up and spit out by life. I hope that you find that dream you have been chasing.*

Evan had managed to escape the building, as he put it, without meeting anyone else. His police shield and police-issue revolver sat on his supervisor's desk. Evan had no intention of picking up either one again, anywhere.

Pulling into a parking lot of a coffee shop in a small town on his way north, Evan parked and turned off the ignition. He faced a drive of about four hours, he thought. *I'm too tired to do this today but something keeps driving me on. No pun intended, dear Lord.*

He brushed at the thick blond hair that he had had cropped short to control the waves in it. His deep gray eyes searched the area out of habit, a habit that he knew he would never lose. He walked back towards his vehicle, setting his coffee into the cup holder in the console and then dropping his bag of food onto the passenger seat. He wasn't hungry, not yet.

A piercing scream and cries of *"leave me alone"* and *"let me go"* rang through the air and Evan spun, searching the area

---

before he was running towards the closed public school beside the coffee shop. He rounded the corner of the building and slid to a halt, just for a moment. He then charged forward, flinging himself into the fray, his weight and sudden appearance taking the two people down.

Evan held the man to the ground even as he watched the female, a lady he realized, around his own age, wiggle out from under the man. Her dark brown eyes were huge and the red hair, or rather copper-coloured hair, was in disarray.

"Run!" Evan's words slashed through the air. "Run! I'll keep him down until you get away. My vehicle is next door. Head for it." He struggled with his captive, his head turning as he watched her scramble to her feet and flee the scene. He faintly heard a car door slam.

His attention went back to the man and he finally stood, releasing him.

"What did you want with her?"

"None of your business." The man, tall and lanky, stood, spinning as he searched for her. "Where'd she go?"

"She's long gone. I asked. What did you want with her?"

"None of your business." The man's fist flew towards Evan, who simply ducked and let it fly harmlessly over his head.

"I'm leaving, man. Control your anger. And I just hope and pray that she never meets you again." Evan backed away until he reached the corner of the school, took one final look at the man, who was approaching menacingly towards him and then turned and ran. He was in his vehicle, driving away before the man had reached the parking lot. His hand held the lady down in the seat, hiding her from sight, his eyes on the fist being shaken in the air behind him.

He finally raised his hand, letting her sit up, even as he drove rapidly from the area and hit the highway, still heading north out of habit. His eyes slashed between the road and his companion, watching as she tried to tidy herself.

"What was that all about?" His words were loud and sounded hoarse. Evan winced. "I'm sorry. I didn't mean to come across like that."

"Well, you did. Find somewhere to drop me off. I'll be okay." Her hand slid up and down the strap on her backpack, belying the confidence that she tried to convey.

"Not happening. Not yet anyway. So, tell me. What was that all about? And start at the beginning, please."

She stared out the side window, not responding. Evan's mouth tightened into a thin line. *Okay, Lord, now what? What have I gotten myself into?*

"I'm Evan Brant. What's your name?" He waited, the road sliding away under the tires, moments ticking by.

"I'm Flannery. Flannery MacTavish." Flannery turned and with a glimpse, he could see the fear in her eyes.

"Hello, Flannery. An unusual name for a beautiful lady." Evan didn't realize what he had said but his words had Flannery's eyes flying to his face, searching for humour or derision but finding neither.

"Thank you. Evan, can you let me off in the next town? Please?"

Evan shook his head. "If he's following you, that's where he would expect you to be." Evan turned his head for a moment. "Where's your car?"

"I don't have one. I was travelling by bus and missed the connection this morning. I don't know who he was but he approached me when I was sitting outside the coffee shop. I tried to run from him. He made me feel so uncomfortable. I ran the wrong way and that's how he trapped me. Thank you."

Evan shrugged, his eyes on the emergency lights coming up behind him.

"Sit tight. Let me do the talking, okay?" Evan pulled to the side of the road, his emergency flashers on as the patrol vehicle stopped behind him.

Flannery's eyes shot to the back window as she watched, and Evan could feel the palpable fear emanating from her.

"Evan?"

Evan turned as he heard his name and grinned.

"Taggart Rafferty. What are you doing stopping me?"

"Your plate was given to us to investigate. I didn't think the caller was legit, nor did anyone else." Tag ducked his head to look over at Flannery, who stared back at him, desperately trying to control her fear. "Someone reported that you had kidnapped someone."

"Me? Not a chance." He slid a sideways glance at Flannery, finding her staring out the side window. "This is a friend, Tag. She was accosted and attacked by a man back there in town. I helped her to escape." He heard her soft sound of disagreement. "We have to tell Tag, Flannery. Otherwise, he'll haul me into town and make me stay there all day. And I don't want that."

"That I would do, miss. Okay, Evan. Description. What all happened?" Tag's notebook and pen were out as he jotted down his notes.

Evan described what he had come upon and then what Flannery had told him. He shook his head slightly at Tag as he opened his mouth to question Flannery. Tag nodded, knowing that Evan had read her right. She would say nothing more to him. It was likely, Tag thought, that Evan had to pry the information from her.

"Okay, Evan. I have your number if I need to call you. You're heading to the hunt camp?"

"I am, Tag. That's my home for the foreseeable future." Evan didn't look at his friend, keeping his eyes trained through the windshield.

Tag was puzzled. He had not heard that Evan had quit, just coming back from his vacation.

"I don't understand, Evan." Tag's voice was puzzled, a frown on his face showing that.

"I've quit the force, Tag. You'll all hear about it later today, I suspect. I asked for a few days to sort myself out and get away. I couldn't handle a goodbye with you all." Evan stared out the windshield. "I'm not coming back, Tag."

"I see. We wondered, Evan, how you were. You disappeared after that incident." Tag was watching Flannery, seeing the puzzlement on her face. "Keep in touch, you hear?"

"I will, Tag. Head up to the cabin when you want to. I'll be around there, or I think I will." Evan's hand reached to flick off the emergency flashers and then set the vehicle into drive, his foot on the accelerator.

Tag nodded before he stepped back to his vehicle, his eyes watching Evan drive away. *Evan,* he muttered, *I have no idea what you've gotten yourself into but that man was angry. Dispatch could hear it. You have made yourself an enemy. He connects with the wrong people and he'll track you down.*

Flannery stared behind her before she stared at Evan.

"What was that all about?"

"Your attacker? He called into dispatch, put out a request for them to find me. He was likely in one of those vehicles that passed us while Tag and I were speaking." Evan turned from the highway. "I'll take the backroad. It will be longer but safer. Not many people know that route. Not the one that I will take."

"I gathered that. But that officer? You seemed to know him well." Flannery turned her gaze towards him, a question on her face.

"I did. We were colleagues. I worked undercover but he was my partner when I first joined the force." He heard her soft exclamation. "I can't walk away from you, Flannery. Not unless and until I know that you are safe. And somehow, I don't think he's done with you. It sounds as if he targeted you. Any idea why?" He shot her a quick glance.

Flannery stared at him. "Targeted me? I don't have any enemies. I have been on the move for months, back and forth across the area. And across the country." She paled. "Has he been following me?"

"Quite likely. From what I know of that small town, that is not what happens there. They watch out for one another. It was very unusual for me to be the only one there in the parking lot. It's a very popular coffee shop."

Flannery paled even more, her hands rubbing up and down her arms as she shuddered.

Evan gave a sound and then reached one hand behind him to rifle around, pulling out a blanket he had tucked there.

"Here. Wrap yourself up in this. We'll talk when I get near my hunt camp and see what we do with you." He didn't expect Flannery to answer, and he was correct in that supposition.

Flannery tucked the blanket around her, even though it was warm in the vehicle. She was suddenly very frightened and cold came with that fear. She had thought someone had been following her the last couple of months, driving her to move

more and more often and to more and more
smaller towns.

Chapter 2

Two hours later, Evan turned into the parking lot of a grocery store. He needed to stock up on food for the camp, not having done that in the town he had walked away from. He had been too afraid that he would run into friends and fellow officers and would have to confess that he was walking away from them all.

Evan tucked the bags of groceries in amongst his belongings in the hatch of his vehicle and carefully pulled the hatch door back down. He looked around, seeming to feel eyes on him, but he wasn't sure. *Maybe I had just worked too much undercover,* he thought. *I feel things when they're not there. Lord, I would ask for peace in this situation. And for protection for Flannery.*

Slipping behind the wheel, Evan glanced over at Flannery, a soft smile creasing his face. She had faded out on him miles past and slept the sleep of someone exhausted and afraid who suddenly felt safe. He turned in his seat, reaching for a small pillow that he carried everywhere he travelled. His hand ran over the worn fabric. His mother had made it for him when he was a toddler. "*Just your size*" had been her words. She had hugged him tight that day. It had not been too long after that when she had died suddenly. A brain aneurysm that had ruptured took her from her beloved husband and son. He had cherished that pillow since then, one of the few things he had that had been his mother's.

He gently lifted Flannery's head and tucked the pillow between it and the window. It would help, Evan thought, to soften the roughness of the road that he would soon be on. He tucked copper-coloured waves behind her ear, the back of his finger resting gently on the bruising on her cheek. Evan could feel the anger growing in him towards the man who had hurt her.

Lord, I don't know why I was there, but You do. I don't know Flannery's story, but You do. You know who that man was and what he wanted. I can only imagine. The life on the street and undercover that I led in the past few years leave little to my imagination. I pray for safety for my new friend, Lord. Let me be Your hands and feet on the ground for her, please, Lord? Evan was not aware that Flannery had already entangled herself around his heartstrings. All he knew was that he could not walk away from anyone in distress, particularly a beautiful lady.

Watching the road around him carefully, Evan finally turned into the lane leading to his new home. Branches tapped along the vehicle as he drove slowly in, the vehicle swaying slightly from the ruts in the road. *I'll need to fill those,* he thought. *A load or two of gravel will do that just fine. And I know who to call.*

Evan parked in his usual spot, his eyes searching. *Everything looked normal,* he thought. *I can see where Everett has been in and out, ensuring everything is safe.* He undid his seatbelt and then turned to Flannery. The same soft smile as before creased his tired, worn face. *I'll let her sleep,* he thought, before he climbed down from his seat.

Stretching, his hands reaching for the sky, Evan breathed in the fresh clean air. He loved this spot. It had belonged to his paternal grandfather and had been passed down to his father, who passed it down to

—

Evan. *We spent a lot of time here, didn't we, Lord? Just Dad and I most of the time. He always said Mom loved this place and had wanted to retire here when the time came. Neither one of them got a chance. Losing Dad to heart disease five years ago changed my life so much. Maybe that's why I spent so much time undercover.*

Emptying the vehicle and stashing away his supplies and belongings, Evan turned. He started his fire in the old cookstove and then laid a new fire ready to be lit in the fireplace. It would be chilly he knew in the evening. Everett would have checked the chimneys for him.

Evan slipped back behind the wheel, his fingers tapping gently on it. He reached for Flannery's arm, giving it a light shake. Only he never once expected her reaction.

Flannery jumped at his touch, a scream echoing through the vehicle as her eyes flew open and she frantically searched for that man.

Evan stared at her, a hand on top of his head. He had jumped at her scream, his head hitting hard.

"What did you do that for?" His eyes were wide with shock as he kept his gaze on her.

"Do what?" Flannery stared back at him, her own eyes huge with fright.

"Scream? You likely sent every critter scurrying for safety."

"You touched me! That's why!"

"I had to. You were sleeping. I needed to awaken you. We're here." He shook his head even as he felt at the tender spot.

"Of course, I screamed. Wouldn't you?" Flannery looked around. "Where are we again?"

"At my hunt camp. We'll stay here tonight. Then, tomorrow, we'll need to figure out what to do with you." He stared at her in shock as she gave a harsh laugh and then sobered, fear flickering in her eyes.

"I told you. You were supposed to just leave me somewhere. I'd be okay."

Evan was out of his seat and around to the passenger's door, yanking it open and then almost pulling her from the vehicle. Despite her protest, he dragged her into the cabin and then shoved her down into a chair. He paced, his eyes on her even as he rubbed at his cheek.

"Evan? What was that for?"

"Flannery. How do I get through to you that you're not safe? Not until we find that man and figure out what he wanted." Evan had an idea but wouldn't express it.

"No. I can leave. I've been on my own for the last fifteen years since I was a teenager. I have spent the last few moving from place to place." She sobered, blinking rapidly at the memories of what she had been through.

Evan crouched down in front of her, his hands reaching for hers, waiting patiently until she placed hers in his before he gently grasped them.

"Flannery? I know that you feel you'll be fine. I don't. Not after what happened. I saw too much, I guess, on the street and when I was undercover. I don't want any harm to come to you. Tag will search for the man. He'll let me know when he finds him. But we don't know who all that man has working for him that might track you down."

"You think that they will?" Her voice was barely above a whisper, so low that Evan had to lean closer to her to understand what she was saying.

"I do. I'm sorry. He wanted something from you or wanted you to do something. Now that he can't do either, he'll be after you. We just have to figure out who he is and why. I don't think that he approached you just because you were there on your own for nothing. He had a reason."

"I know." Flannery looked up at the ceiling, blinking back the tears of fear that she refused to shed. "I think someone was following me the last few months. Only I never saw them. Just felt watched. And sometimes, if I left my pack in my room, it would seem that it had been searched. I moved on every time that happened."

Evan watched with compassion before he nodded and rose, heading for the kitchen. He squinted at the clock. Time for a meal, he thought. Something simple for tonight. He heard Flannery moving around quietly and then the click of the bathroom door before he heard the water running.

Chapter 3

Flannery stood watching Evan as he moved around the kitchen. Not many men she knew would be that comfortable making a meal, she thought. She had had a shower, something that she had felt she had needed and dressed in clean clothes. Her hair she had simply pulled back into a clip, knowing that she couldn't stand the wet hair on her neck.

Evan turned as he heard her soft footsteps, a smile of welcome on his face before he pointed to the couch in front of the fireplace. He had lit a fire, the air in the cabin chilly.

"We can eat there, Flannery." He lifted a tray and headed that way, waiting until she was seated before he set it down on the rough table that sat in front of the couch. "We'll eat. And then I would like to pray with you."

"You pray?" Flannery's eyes shot up to him even as he sat beside her.

"I do, Flannery. No matter what I have done or not done, no matter where I have been, I pray. God is Who has kept me alive. My father instilled the habit of prayer in everything when I was just young, just after Mom died."

Flannery opened her mouth and then snapped it closed. She would ask later, she thought, bowing her head, hearing his prayer for the food to be blessed to them and for protection for herself. She frowned slightly. She didn't think God heard prayers anymore. He certainly had ignored hers over the years, her prayers for stability, for somewhere to call her own. Instead, she had been on the move, constantly, not staying more than a month or two in one spot. Flannery decided at that point that she was very tired of the nomadic lifestyle and knew what her dream was. Only her dream of a loving husband, children, and home likely would never come to fruition.

Handing her the plate of stew that he had prepared, Evan ate at his own food, his mind on the man who had accosted her. He frowned, a thought nudging at him. He had been warned about a man doing just this, finding women and teens to run drugs and goods for him. Was that what he had wanted? He sent his plate down and reached for his mug.

"I wasn't sure what you liked to drink."

"Coffee is fine, for tonight. Do you have tea or juice crystals?" Flannery didn't look up at him, her concentration on the last few bites of food on her plate.

"There's tea. Dad liked his tea and I have always kept it fresh, even though he's gone. Juice crystals? No, I don't have them. I do have juice."

"It's okay. I like juice crystals in hot water. Don't ask me why. Someone started me off on that." Flannery's gaze went to the fireplace and she barely felt him remove her plate from her hand.

Evan gathered up their dishes, heading to put them to soak, his mind working on what Flannery's life must have been like. He turned, drying his hands on a towel that he hung carefully back up on its hook. He watched Flannery as she curled up in the corner of the couch, her hand holding her mug and her eyes on the fire. The light from the flames flickered across her face. He had a sudden vision of Flannery sitting there for the rest of their lives and he stopped short as he made to

---

move from the counter. Evan shook his head. *There is no way, Lord, that she would be here. I'm committed to being single all my life, remember? I saw the hurt that Dad tried hard to hide after losing Mom. I don't know that I could go through that.* Evan paused. *Okay, Lord, I hear You. I'll leave that unspoken dream open if You insist. But I don't expect it to happen.*

Flannery turned her head as Evan sat back down, his refreshed mug of coffee hitting the table. He turned to watch her, a shuttered look on his face that disturbed her.

"Evan?"

Evan sighed. "Flannery? What am I to do with you? We need to find somewhere you'll be safe."

"Just take me to the nearest town where there's a bus. I'll leave." She kept her eyes on her mug.

"I can't do that, Flannery. Not with having seen what you faced. It's not in me to walk away from a lady. Not while I am still breathing."

"And if you're not? What happens if he comes back and kills you?" Flannery was horrified at that thought.

———

31

Evan shrugged. "I've faced worse. In case you missed it, I was a police officer. Undercover or working the streets the last few years."

It was Flannery's turn to watch Evan with compassion on her face.

"It chewed you up and spit you out, as my mother would have said. And you're on the run, trying to make sense of everything. You've gone into hiding."

Evan stared at her. She had pinpointed exactly what he was doing.

"That's correct. This place? It's my haven. Dad made it that way. We lost my Mom when I was small. It was just Dad and I for so many years until I lost him a few years ago. We would retreat to here, spend weekends or holidays here, making memories, he would say. Those memories are what I am hoping will help me get back."

"You'll never be back to that person, Evan." Flannery's eyes went back to the fire. Her voice softened as she spoke once more. "You never will. Life has gotten in the way. It has changed you from that person to who you are. Don't let your experiences harden you."

"You've seen that," Evan spoke with conviction.

"I did. My own father. He had some very bad experiences with people. That made him bitter. That bitterness led to his finding alcohol. He died in a motor vehicle accident, driving while intoxicated. Thankfully no one else was hurt. But the first responders? They have to deal with that death. It changes them."

"You are a very wise lady, Flannery. One I would like to call my friend." He squinted through the dimness at the clock. "It's getting late. You take the bunk in the bedroom. I'll be fine out here."

She rose, her eyes on him before she nodded.

"Thank you. We'll talk in the morning."

His hand on her wrist stopped her for a moment as he looked up at her.

"I pray that you won't need it. There is a hollow between the bed and the wall. Just enough to fit a person. The mattress pulls back over it. You can hide there if you need to. Dad made it for me, just as a gag, he said, but it became a place where I could go and pray and cry when I was young."

"Thank you, Flannery. And thank you to your father for being such a wonderful parent." She moved away, her hand reaching for her backpack. Once in the bedroom, she turned to study the closed door before her pack was hung in the closet.

Lord, I have no idea what is coming, but they tell me that You do. That You are in control. Protect that man out there, if that's the only thing that I can ask?

Evan rose, his eyes on the closed door before he tidied the kitchen for the night. He stepped outside, his eyes becoming accustomed to the moonlight that filtered through the surrounding trees. He made his rounds, ensuring that everything was well for the night. He stood on the front porch, his eyes on the sky, silent communication with his God before he nodded and entered the cabin, seeking the sleeping bag that he had spread out in front of the dying fire.

Chapter 4

Rising early the next morning, Evan made his coffee and then headed around the cabin to the back. He needed to chop wood and made short work of that, carrying in an armful and dropping it into the wood box. He reached to refill his coffee, pausing as he heard a vehicle.

It's early for visitors, he thought. *Maybe Everett has come around.* He peeked through the window by the door and sighed. *Of course, it would be that man. He had to find me, now didn't he?*

Stepping outside the door and pulling it closed behind him, he prayed that Flannery would awaken and make use of the hiding place. He didn't want her falling into this man's hands again.

"Can I help you? You're on private property. That road is private." Evan's voice had the four men spinning to stare at him.

The man from the day before nodded.

"You have the lady. She's mine. Bring her out."

"Not happening. She doesn't belong to anyone." Evan set his mug on the windowsill, knowing that a fight was likely coming, and he needed his hands free.

"She is. She works for me. So, bring her out." When Evan just stood there, the man motioned to one of his men. "If you don't, a nice fire at this time of the morning would be welcome."

Evan watched as the second man reached for a branch and then pulled out his lighter. *This is it, isn't it, Lord?* He threw himself at the man, arms around the other man's waist, taking him down. His fist landed on the man's chin and he noted with satisfaction that the man lay still.

His wrists and upper arms were grasped in hard, tight holds and Evan was hauled to his feet. Standing facing the leader of the men, he simply waited, knowing that any reaction would lead to further violence. *Only there is no way I'm avoiding that, is there?*

The leader stared at Evan before he opened his mouth.

"Where is she? We know she was with you. We saw her."

Evan remained silent, his eyes watchful, looking for any opportunity to escape. He shook his head at the man's repeated questions. The leader nodded at the man that Evan had tackled. A hard-knotted fist drove into Evan's jaw, sending his head jerking backwards in an abrupt manner. Blood trickled from the lip that he had bitten.

Evan still refused to speak. Moments later, he lay sprawled face down on the ground, not moving. No matter the blows or words that had been directed his way, he had refused to speak. He had kept his face blank, knowing that the character of the man in front of him would delight even more at any revelation of pain on Evan's part.

The three men separated, searching Evan's vehicle and the cabin. They returned, shaking their heads.

"She's not here. There is no sign of her ever being here."

"She has to be. He didn't leave last night. And she was in the vehicle, wasn't she when he turned in here?" The leader spun in a circle, curses flying from his mouth before he stomped to his vehicle and into it. "Let's go. Let's see where we can find her."

Flannery had awakened as she heard the loud angry shouts and had raised herself. Creeping to the window, she had watched horrified as Evan had been hauled to his feet and restrained from moving away from the men. *This is because of me,* she thought, her head flipping around as she frantically sought somewhere to hide. She ran for the bunk, tidying it up as much as she could, reaching for her sneakers and slipping into them. Her pack? She prayed that it would be safe where it was. Flannery had searched the night before to find the hiding spot. She had even slipped into it, to make sure it fit her and that she knew how to work the mattress if she had to. She had smiled at the cloth handle sewed roughly on the bottom of the mattress. *He really did do this for you, didn't he, Evan? Such a wonderful caring father.*

She swiftly straightened the covers and then slid the mattress over enough that she could drop into the area, the mattress pulled back over her. She raised it enough to reach out one hand and straighten the bedding hanging down as best she could.

———

Barely breathing, Flannery had listened to the heavy footsteps of the men as they searched for her, the doors to the closets opening and closing. She heard the anger in their words even though she could not hear what they were saying. She breathed a sigh of relief as she heard the door slam closed behind them.

She waited, knowing that the men might still be out there. Finally, Flannery shoved back the mattress and slid from her hiding spot, pulling the mattress back in place. She cautiously snuck to the window, pulling the curtain to one side just enough to be able to see out.

They're gone, Lord, but where is Evan? Did they take him with them? She flew through the cabin and out of the door, her footsteps stopping as she reached the edge of the porch. An arm came out to wrap around a post as she barely caught herself from flying forward. A hand covered her mouth as she stared down at Evan's unmoving body.

Chapter 5

Running towards where Evan lay, Flannery's breath caught in her throat as she feared that he had been killed. She was on her knees, trying her best to turn him to his back, finally managing that, her fear lending strength to her hands. She cradled him in her arms, her right hand seeking for a pulse. Head dropping as she breathed a sigh of relief, she gently touched the cuts and bruising that was appearing on his face. Blood trickled from his split lip and a cut above his eyebrow.

She looked around, knowing that she had to get him inside, but knowing that she couldn't pick up him. She finally rose, her hands under his arms and dragged him. It was hard work, but she didn't stop. Flannery paused as she reached the three steps. It pained her knowing that she would cause more pain for him by dragging him up the steps and across the porch. But she had no other option, not that she could see. She didn't think that there were neighbours close enough to run to. Not out in the woods as they were.

Flannery sighed, steeled herself and gently or as gently as she could pulled Evan up the steps and across the porch. She shoved at the partly open door with her hip and watched as it swung back to hit the small table resting behind it.

Finally settling Evan down on his still open sleeping bag, Flannery sat back. Her breath came in gasps and pants. She was not used to dragging a man across the area that she had, she decided. He was tall, she thought, over six feet. But not stocky. That he worked out regularly showed.

She was on her feet, running for hot water and searching through the cupboards for cloths. She set the basin down on the floor and then flew to the bathroom, searching for a first aid kit. Flannery grasped it, holding it high in victory. *Thank you, Lord. Now, let's see what You and I can do with this.* She didn't realize that her prayers had changed. She was praying once more, asking for help, not crying out in anger and frustration as had been her wont for the last few years.

Dropping to her knees, Flannery dunked the cloth into the warm water and then gently began to bathe Evan's face. She knew only the basics of first aid and feared that he had been hurt badly. She could only do so much. She refused to call for help, praying that he would awaken and tell her that he was okay.

A tap at the open door had her on her feet, terrified, a hand to her throat. A man entered through the open door and paused as he saw her.

"You're not Evan." Everett Summerfield stood watching her closely.

"No, I'm not. I'm a friend, I guess. He's been hurt." Flannery was back on her knees, trying to assess Evan's condition and failing miserably at it.

"He has?" Everett was on his knees as well. Flannery never knew how he crossed the room so quickly and so quietly. "What happened?"

"He helped me yesterday. The man who tried to abduct me or whatever it was he tried appeared this morning. He had three men with him. They beat him up."

"He wouldn't tell them where you were. They searched the cabin?" Everett shot a look at her from his keen eyes.

Flannery nodded her head, not too sure on how much to say.

"You found the hiding spot. Good. Evan would have told you, knowing him. Now, let's see what we can do for him."

Everett finally rose, his eyes on Flannery as he did so. *She had not flinched,* he thought, no matter how he had probed and prodded at Evan, eliciting groans from the younger man. *Good. He needs her in his life.*

Flannery's hand rested on Evan's hands that lay on his abdomen. She had watched Everett closely, trying to remember what all he had done and knowing that she just wouldn't. Blood never bothered her. At least, not until now. She had cringed to herself as the basin's water had coloured pink and then darker and had risen to fetch fresh water without Everett's asking her to.

Everett puttered in the kitchen, making tea, sweetening the cup that he would hand to Flannery. She needed it, he thought, her face pale from shock.

Flannery spluttered out the mouthful of tea that she had just taken, staring at her mug and then at Everett.

—

"I don't drink sweetened tea." She started to rise, to dump it out and make herself a fresh mug. Everett's hand on her shoulder kept her still.

"I didn't think that you did, at least not that sweet. You need it, young lady. Your adrenalin is fading. The sugar will help." He shook his head at her. "Drink it and I promise. I'll make you another one."

Everett perched on the edge of the stones around the hearth. He watched Evan closely. *He's been hurt, dear Lord, has he not? To protect this lovely young lady. I wonder how connected his heart is to her. Knowing Evan, he will fall and fall quickly. His father and I often spoke about who he would marry, especially in those last months. I promised Ian I would look out for him and I shall.*

"Everett?" Flannery's voice had his head raising as he looked across at her. "How is he? Really?"

"Really? That I'm not sure of. He has some bruised ribs, but I don't think they're fractured. Bruising in the abdomen, but again I don't think there's internal harm. He's taken a beating. Has a concussion more than likely. You see the cuts and bruises."

"I know. That worries me. How can he manage if he has a concussion?" Flannery chewed at her lower lip, a habit that she was trying hard to break, one that only came out when she was really worried or scared.

"We'll manage. Eunice and I will be here, one or the other of us. By the way, I'm a retired paramedic."

"You are? That's how you knew what to do. Are you friends?" Flannery sat back, her legs tucked under her. Her eyes rested on Evan.

"We are. Once he's on his feet, I'll take you both to our cabin. It's right next door." Everett pointed to the far side of the cabin. "It's not that far between us. Evan wore a path there when he was young, and the path still gets used. That's how I got here today."

"You can't carry him. And he's not going to be able to walk."

Everett grinned. "No, I can't and no, he won't. We'll use his car. You can walk over if you like." A small grin hovered on his face.

Flannery looked up in shock before her brows lowered. "I will do no such thing.

—

If he goes in his vehicle, so do I. What should I pack for him?"

"Let me, Flannery." Everett was on his feet, hunting for clothes and whatnot that he knew Evan would want. "What about you?"

"All I own fits into my backpack. I'll just bring it."

Flannery didn't see the compassionate look that Everett turned her way. He had no idea what her story was, but Evan was involved in it. That was enough for Everett and he knew it would be enough for Eunice.

Chapter 6

Standing on his feet, as wobbly as he was, Evan felt rocky. His head hurt and he had glared at Everett when he laughed at him, saying of course it would. He had been beaten, didn't he remember?

"Of course, I remember. I was there, wasn't I?" He felt Flannery's hand on his own wrist of the arm that she had pulled around her shoulders to help him stand. "Where did you come from, Everett?"

"I came in just after your young lady pulled you into the cabin, she tells me." Everett didn't miss the look on Evan's face as he stared down at Flannery through blurry eyes. "Now, we've packed up what we need for the next few days. We're heading back to my place. Flannery informs me that she plans on walking there." Everett grinned at her, his sense of humour coming into play. He shook his head slightly at Flannery.

"I am doing no such thing!" Flannery played along with Everett, their combined forces ready to help Evan and to do battle for him if need be. "I told you. He's in the vehicle, I'm in the vehicle."

"All right then. Here, Evan. Let me help you. I have your keys as it's the one we'll be using."

"Walked over, did you? Surprised to find us here?"

"No, not really. Sam alerted us to the fact that we had company late last night. So I figured you were here." Sam was Everett's Australian shepherd, a dog that loved Evan and could hardly wait for Evan to step into sight before he was jumping all over him, licking as fast as his tongue would move.

"He did?" Evan's eyes closed as he was maneuvered down the steps, the pain jarring through him. "I'm okay, guys. Let's get settled."

"I'm sure you are. And you'll tell me that you have been hurt worse before. This time, Evan, you're not where you can get ready medical help. And you have a young lady worried very badly about you." Everett shut the door after Evan, watching his young friend.

—

"Everett? Did we hurt him more?" Flannery was worried, even as she kept looking around, waiting for that man as she called him to appear.

"No, I don't suppose we did. In you get, young lady. We'll let Eunice take a look at him. And then she'll want to know all the details of why and how." Everett had not informed Flannery that his wife was a retired officer and still kept in touch with her colleagues while working for the local town constabulary.

"She will? Why?" Flannery's seatbelt was fastened even as she leaned forward to watch Evan.

"She's a retired officer, Flannery. She can help with this."

"Oh! Did God do this?"

"Do what, child?" Everett turned for a moment to watch her face, seeing the quietness and questioning on it.

"Bring me here. Get Evan involved. Bring you and your wife into my life?" Flannery stared out the side window of the truck, not wanting to see the pity she imagined would be on Everett's face.

"I suspect that He did. You needed help and He provided that help. We'll talk, child. We will talk, that I promise you. But first, we see to Evan and then Eunice will want to mother you. Our daughter is overseas right now for work and she misses her."

"She's not married?"

"She's engaged. I suspect that she's about your age. They are planning to marry in the fall." Everett pulled to a stop near the cabin. "This is home, Flannery. Welcome to it. It's humble but the love we feel for our friends and family makes it a castle."

"Thank you, Everett. I have not had a home in so many years, I've forgotten what it is like."

Evan roused as Everett helped him from the vehicle and then up the stairs, a hand wrapping around his abdomen. Eunice was there, pointing towards one of the spare rooms.

"In there, sweetheart. Evan, who did you tangle with?"

"I need to talk to you, Eunice, but I don't think that I can stay awake long enough to. Flannery can tell you about it." Everett closed the door and then helped Evan to the bed, pulling the covers over his

---

friend. His sneakers were set neatly on the floor near the end of the bed.

Eunice turned to Flannery, finding the younger woman standing with her arms wrapped around herself, her backpack resting on the floor at her feet. She took pity on her, the uncertainty and fear that she felt drawing her towards her.

"And you would be?"

"Flannery MacTavish, ma'am. Is Evan okay?" Flannery's eyes sought the closed door.

"He's in good hands, Flannery. May I call you that?" Eunice's arm was around her, drawing her to the kitchen. "Have you eaten?"

"Everett made me. He also made me drink a horrible cup of sweetened tea." Flannery grimaced at the memory.

Eunice began to laugh, drawing Flannery's eyes to her.

"It's okay. It's an old remedy that he likes to use. It worked, didn't it?"

"He says it did. It stopped my shaking, so I guess he was right."

"I was, was I?" Everett grinned as he watched her jump. "Sorry, Flannery. I'll wear a bell so that you hear me coming. Eunice is always complaining that I'm too quiet."

"You are, dear. Here. I have soup that was just ready when you came in. Flannery, sit. This meal, you're company. Then we put you to work." Eunice had their meal on the table in short order, seating herself and then reaching for hands. "We hold hands when we ask the blessing."

"That's wonderful. Mom did that with me." Flannery blinked at the memory.

Chapter 7

Evan was on his feet by that evening, rocky still at times, but refusing to stay in bed. He had simply folded Flannery into his arms, holding to her tightly as she had wept when she saw him. He knew that her emotions were likely all over the place. His were.

Everett had watched before a hand on Evan's back had directed him to the living room. It looked out over the dock and lake, the setting sun sending its long pink and purple rays shooting into the room. The open windows let in a light breeze as well as the sounds of the settling day birds and insects and the activity of the night critters as Evan called them.

Evan sank down gratefully onto the couch, an arm around her bringing Flannery down with him. He landed harder than he expected, a groan coming from him.

"Evan?" Flannery's voice held worry.

"I'm okay, love. I'm okay."

Flannery's eyes had widened at what he had called her. *He didn't mean that. I know he didn't.*

"What happened?"

"Your friend showed up as did three other men. They didn't take it well when I stopped one from setting fire to my home. They also didn't like it when I refused to tell them where you were. Found the hiding place?" Evan squinted as he watched her face.

"I did. I was so afraid when I looked out and saw them. I thought that you were dead."

"It takes a lot to put me down. Everett, thanks for helping me into the cabin." Evan stared at Everett as the older man began to laugh. "What did I say?"

"Your young lady did that. She says that she pulled you into the house, dragging you is how she put it. That she couldn't very well pick you up and carry you, now could she?" Everett grinned at Flannery as she frowned at him. "It's what you said, child. Isn't it?"

"It is. I didn't mean to drag him. I didn't have a choice. I couldn't leave him out there." Flannery was close to tears, her remembered fear uppermost in her mind.

Evan's arm tightened around her. "And I didn't feel a thing. That much I know. I understand, love. It's okay." He looked at Eunice who had set a tray down beside him and then claimed her chair, her eyes on him. "Eunice. I know that look."

She grinned at her young friend. "I know you do. You've given it many times yourself, I have no doubt. Eat your soup and then we'll talk. I still have resources that I can call on."

"Talk to Tag Rafferty. He stopped me on the way up yesterday. The man had called them, saying Flannery had been kidnapped and by me." Evan gave a concise summary of what had happened, in between spoonfuls of the beef soup, thick with barley and vegetables. "This is good, Eunice. I have missed your soup."

"It was warm today, but I felt like soup. Everett eats whatever I set before him. Most days. Today, his thoughts were on you and your young lady."

"Why?" Flannery stared around at the three.

Everett grinned at her. "Why what?"

"What do you call me Evan's young lady? I'm not!"

Everett's grin widened. "But you are. For now. It's how we can introduce you without questions being raised. You see, Flannery, it's like this." Everett leaned forward, his hands clasped as his arms rested on his thighs. His grin had disappeared as he sobered. "We are a close-knit community here. Evan and his father are part of it. At least, his father was one of the founding members of our community board. We watch out for one another. Strangers are welcomed but held at arms' lengths. We watch them and consider what they want. It is based on long evidence of trouble with some strangers. If you are here as a friend or as Evan's young lady, you will be welcome. The community will envelop you into their midst. They will watch out for you. All we have to do is put word and the description out and those men will be followed, detained if necessary, by our local constabulary. They will do everything they can to make you stay safe."

"They would do that for me? A stranger? Just because of Evan?" Flannery didn't quite know how to word her feelings, surprise high on her list of emotions.

"They will. Flannery, we can't stay together at the cabin. That's a given. Last night? We got away with it just because it was late. But not now. Everett has offered to have you stay here with them." Evan raised a hand at her protest. "It's what they do, Flannery. It's who they are. Eunice is part of our constabulary if that's what you want to call it. We have four or five that work that. We don't need a lot. Everett is part of training our paramedics and search and rescue personnel. Sam there? He's a search dog. He knows you now." Sam's head had raised as he heard his name, and he gave a short bark of agreement.

"I see. I didn't expect that." Flannery settled back against Evan, not realizing that he still had his arm around her. "I guess God led me here."

"He did, Flannery. Make no mistake about that. I would suspect that you have been running for the last few months. Am I correct?" Eunice's look of compassion almost broke Flannery's stern wall of reserve. At her nod, Eunice shared a look with Everett. "We'll talk, child. You can tell me what all you have faced. Evan can

be a part of the discussion if you wish. I
know that he'll want to be. We both have
resources and friends that we can call in to
assist you."

Chapter 8

Two days later, Evan paused as he approached his own cabin. His hand rested on Sam's head, stopping the dog. He sighed. They've been around again, haven't they, Lord? He moved forward cautiously, his eyes searching. Sam's hackles were raised, and he forged ahead, searching for the enemies that he sensed. He returned to Evan's side, content to be there after his search.

Evan entered his cabin, seeing nothing wrong or missing. He searched carefully, not finding anything awry. He paused in the centre of the living room.

"They were here, Sam. The door was unlocked. The lock had been picked. I know Everett would have locked it behind them." He reached for a bag to pack more clothes. Eunice had insisted that he continue to stay with them until he was better. He had stared at her, not missing the shuttered look to her face or the glance that she gave Flannery.

—

59

"Flannery needs me, doesn't she, Sam?" Evan locked the door behind him and headed towards the forest, stopping at the paper tacked to a tree that was waving in the wind. He reached for it, a grim look on his face as he read it.

"Where is she? She had something that I want. She is mine. I will find her, and you will pay the price for keeping us apart."

"Not very subtle is he." Evan frowned. "The wording sounds familiar." He reached for his phone, a quick photo taken and sent it on to Tag. "He'll look into, I know, Sam. Let's head for your home and your people. And yes, Flannery."

Sam's tail began to wag as he heard Flannery's name. He had claimed the young lady, not straying far from her side if he could at all help it.

Flannery met him halfway back. She had been away with Eunice to their small town. Eunice had insisted that she need to buy things for a friend, Flannery not aware that she was the friend until they were on their way home. She had protested but Eunice had just shaken her head and told her to accept them from God. Flannery had stared at her, finally nodding.

She had gone looking for Evan, dismayed that he had headed back to his own cabin. Everett had pointed out the way for her, following at a distance until he saw Evan. A hand was raised to the younger man before he turned and walked back home.

"Evan?" Flannery's voice held the question that she wouldn't ask him. Not yet, as she felt she didn't know him well enough.

"I'm okay, love. I'm okay." He reached for her hand, not really understanding that he had, and clasped hers tight in his. She looked askance at their hands and then shrugged. What could it hurt? "We need to talk. I found a note on a tree."

Flannery sighed. "He's been back, hasn't he? He just won't stop."

"No, he won't. And we need to stop him. First, we need to find out who he is and that's something I have asked Tag to look into. I know Eunice is as well. But for now, let's head for the dock. Have you been down there yet?" He set his pack on the back steps and then led her to the dock. "Everett has a boat, canoes and kayaks. Do you swim?"

"I do but not well. I have never been in either a canoe or kayak." She stared out across this lake. "This is nice. I don't know how you could leave it to live in the city."

Flannery dropped down on the end of the dock, copying Evan's motions in removing her sneakers. He dropped beside her, an arm around her to keep her in place as she tried to shift away. Sam plopped down beside her, his paw on her knee.

"I said we need to talk. But not right now."

"I think so. I can't enjoy this if you keep me in suspense." Flannery bit at her lip. "He wants me, doesn't he?"

"He does but he also said that you had something of his. Know anything about that?"

Flannery shook her head. "I have so little. I would know if I had something that wasn't mine." She sighed. "At least I had little until today. Eunice insisted on shopping for a friend. She just didn't tell me that I was the friend."

Evan laughed. "She does that, Flannery. It's how she is the hands and feet of God. Helping others in need. She always has."

"That's what she said." Flannery continued to bite at her lip. "I don't get it, Evan. What could he possibly want?"

"If he's into drugs, he may want you to serve as a mule." He watched her face. "Do you know what that is?"

"Someone who transports drugs." She sighed. "I can't do that. At least not willingly or knowing that's what I was doing."

"I know. We'll work on that. Now, about you. Where do you want to be?" Evan looked out over the lake, not wanting to see the rejection on her face. She was becoming important to him, her feistiness a refreshing change from the single ladies who tried so hard to catch his attention.

"I don't know. This is where I could see myself, but I need to work. And there doesn't seem to be much here."

"Eunice will put you to work. She's working on a book of her experiences as an officer. She has been looking for someone to transcribe that. Do you type?"

"I do, but I'm not sure I would be accurate enough."

—

"It's okay. She has a word processing program that you would use. I like that idea, you staying here."

Everett watched the young couple, turning his head as Eunice approached. His arm went out to sweep her close to him as he kissed his wife.

"They're falling in love, Everett." Eunice's voice was quiet.

"I know that they are. What do we know about Flannery's past?"

"She has talked some. Her father was an alcoholic and was killed in an accident. Her mother? Flannery didn't say much but I got the impression that she committed suicide before that happened. Flannery has been on the move and on the run ever since. She told me that she doubts God hears her prayers."

"That's what I thought. We'll pray her back. Evan is moving her that way just from how he is acting. His prayers will work that too."

"I know." Eunice sighed again. "She didn't want to take the clothes and other items. She insisted that she should pay for what I bought her. She was in tears as she fought me on it."

—

"I know. That's her character. Say, you were looking for someone to transcribe your book. How about Flannery?"

Eunice nodded. "That's what I was thinking. It would keep her here and we could watch out for her and for Evan both."

"He's not going to let her go. Not without a fight. He hasn't said much about the other day, but I suspect that he didn't say much if anything at all."

"No, he wouldn't. Now, about supper. You up to grilling?"

"I am. Lead the way, sweetheart."

Chapter 9

A week later, Evan looked up from the porch that he was repairing and squinted as he heard a vehicle. He reached behind him for the sturdy stick that he had started carrying with him before he set it aside, a smile lighting his face.

"Tag!" He walked towards his friend, reaching out to shake his hand. "What brings you up here?"

"A holiday? A weekend away?" Tag grinned before he sobered. "What did you do? How many doors did you walk into?"

"A couple. Come on it. I have coffee on. Eunice and Everett will expect us for supper. Can you stay?"

"I can. I'm up for a couple of days if you can put me up." Tag followed Evan into the cabin, his eyes searching the room. "Where's your lady?"

"With Eunice. She's taken Flannery under her wing, to put it one way.

Flannery's working to transcribe Eunice's handwritten notes on her book."

"She's going ahead with that? Good. I want a copy." Tag pulled out a chair at the table, setting down his mug of coffee. "We need to talk, Evan."

"I'm sure we do, but we need Flannery to be part of it. I promised her that I would not leave her out of anything." Evan stared at his friend. "You're not just here for a vacation."

Tag sighed before he shook his head. "I'm not. You know me too well, Evan. I have a name on the man. He's brutal."

"I know that. I found that out firsthand." Evan glanced at the clock. "We can head over there in about an hour. Your vehicle is safe enough here. Tell me what you have been up to."

An hour later, Flannery glanced up from her computer and smiled, the smile to welcome Evan lighting up her whole face. She had grown accustomed to him being around her and missed him when he wasn't. She looked past him and frowned.

"You remember Tag?" Evan grinned as he reached to hug her, drawing her to her feet, his arm still around her as he asked his question.

"I do. Still stopping innocent motorists?"

Tag stared at her before he shouted with laughter.

"Not forgiving me?" He continued to laugh as she smirked. "You have a live one here, Evan."

"I do. Flannery, Tag is up for a few days, but he has some information that he wants to go over with us."

"He can but after supper. I promised Everett I would help him and I need to do just that." Flannery was away before Evan could stop her.

Tag continued to grin at the look on Evan's face.

"She's a live one as I said, Evan."

That evening, the five gathered around the fireplace in the living room. It had turned into a damp evening and the flames and warmth were welcome. Flannery was seated beside Eunice, Evan seated at her feet. Everett simply bowed his head and began to pray.

Tag finally looked at Evan before he reached for a folder and handed it over. He didn't have to say anything. Evan read his eyes and face.

"This is it, Flannery. We'll take a look at what Tag has brought us. Then we'll likely need to make some decision."

She nodded, her eyes on the paperwork as Evan leafed through it.

"Him? He's that bad and dangerous?" Her eyes were huge with shock.

"He is, Flannery." Tag leaned forward. "He's a known drug lord. We think that he was planning on using you to run drugs for him. How he would manage that, we don't know for sure. But given your looks, you would have been able to get away with it, most likely. It may have been that he would have asked you to deliver innocent-looking packages which would have contained drugs. He has done that in the past, we know, but we have never been able to bring charges against him. The ones that he has used have taken jail time rather than speak out against him. His threats are that bad."

"I see." Flannery grew quieter as the talk went on around her.

Eunice watched her closely before she spoke.

"Flannery? Talk with me. Tell me what you are thinking."

"I am thinking that I brought trouble to all of you, especially Evan. I shouldn't have come." She was on her feet, running from the room, Sam beside her.

Evan was on his feet to follow when Everett stopped him.

"Let me, Evan. Maybe she'll open up more to an old guy."

$$Chapter\ 10$$

Everett lowered his head for a moment before he approached Flannery who had seated herself at the end of the dock. He sat beside her, not saying anything before he began to pray aloud for her.

Flannery wiped at the tears on her cheeks. She wondered that it was Everett and not Evan who had come after her.

"Evan was coming after you. I told him to let me. That maybe you'd speak with an old guy instead."

"You're not old, Everett."

"I feel it some days. This old world? It's full of decay. God knows that. He allows it. Tell me, Flannery. What is your dream?"

"My dream? What kind of a question is that?" She stared at him, not sure what he was asking.

"We all have dreams. Mine was to be a paramedic. I did that. Eunice? Hers was to be a police officer. She has dreams of grandkids but is okay if that doesn't happen. She has this dream of a book and you're helping her with that. So, again my question. What is your dream?"

Flannery nodded, a sober look on her face. "I hear what you're asking. I think I let all my dreams die over the years. I didn't see a point in hanging onto them. They would never have come to fruition."

"But they could. What is one dream that you had?"

"Me? I wanted to help people. I'm not sure what I really had in mind, but that was the intent. To do something that could help people. And poetry. I used to write poetry, but I let that die. I just didn't have the energy to write."

"You do now. Go back to your poetry. As to helping people? You do that just by being you. You're helping in ways that you wouldn't have dreamt of." Everett grew silent. "Now, about what Tag brought to you."

"That. He scares me, Everett, in ways that I have never ever been scared of."

"That's good. Then you'll stay alert. Memorize his face. The face of those he has working for him. If you see any of them, hide. Find someone who will help you. Evan will be on the watch, that much I know of him."

"I know. I am afraid for him." Flannery's voice was barely audible, and she swiped at the tears on her cheeks.

"You love him?" Everett's voice was equally quiet.

"I don't know, Everett. Until I met you two, I wasn't even sure what true love was like." She looked up at the darkening sky. "Mom stayed with Dad. She said that she loved him, but I couldn't understand how she could."

"I can't speak for your parents, nor can you, Flannery. You need to examine your own heart and decide if you are in love with Evan and if he is in love with you and where you both go from here. He will not walk away from you. Not while you're facing what you are. It's not in him as a former officer and it is not in him as the man that he is." Everett rose. "Come in when you're ready. I wouldn't stay out too long though."

Flannery was on her feet, walking back with him.

"I'm not safe, am I?"

Everett shook his head. "I would say not. Evan and Eunice have both said that Sam has been acting unusual, more on guard. That means that someone is around who shouldn't be. If you are out and about, take Sam with you."

Evan was waiting for her as she walked across to the back deck and into the arms that he opened to hug her tight. He didn't say a word, just letting his silence let her know that he understood and cared.

"Tag said he would leave the paperwork. He's heading back to my place. He'll be around for a couple of days."

"I'm sorry, Evan. I shouldn't have run."

"No, you should have. You are afraid and sometimes you have to run to find out what you need to do. All I ask is this. Run to me, sweetheart. Just run to me." He finally turned them to walk into the cabin, finding Eunice just pouring out their coffee and tea.

"All right, Flannery?" Eunice turned, concern on her face. Everett had not said

what the two of them had talked about, but
she hadn't expected it.

"I am, thank you, Eunice. What can I
do to help you?"

Chapter 11

Tag shook his head the next day. Flannery is on a roll, he thought. She had been teasing Evan relentlessly, leaving Evan speechless at times. Everett had watched, a huge grin on his face. Eunice had disappeared, saying that she would be back later.

"It is so." Flannery pointed at that lake. "It's cold."

"No, it's not cold. You just don't understand cold and hot." Evan stood at the end of the dock, back to the lake, taunting Flannery.

"Oh, I understand. Where's your phone?" Her hand was out for it. "Empty your pockets, buster." Her fingers wiggled as she waited.

Tag's grin grew as Evan did that, a puzzled look on his face, handing his belongings to Flannery.

"Why do I need to empty my pockets?" He looked up at Flannery just as her hand landed on his chest and shoved. With a cry, he flew backwards into the lake, disappeared and then surfaced, to find her standing grinning at him. His arms moved in the water as his legs kicked to keep him afloat.

"So, it is hot or cold?" She danced back from the edge as he approached and pulled himself out.

"It's both. I think you need to test it out." He approached her, a grin on his face.

Flannery gave a shriek of laughter and ran, hiding behind Everett and peeking around him.

"You'll protect me, won't you?"

Everett was laughing almost too hard to respond.

"I shouldn't but I'll help a damsel in distress. Evan, she got you on that one."

Evan laughed as well. "She did. I'll be back as soon as I change. Flannery, watch out. One day, it will be your turn."

Flannery stuck her tongue out at him and he stared at her in disbelief as the other two men laughed even harder.

"You need to give up while you're ahead, my friend." Tag stopped beside him. "You'll never win."

"Oh, I think I will. One day. Soon. Maybe." Evan walked away to laughter, his own face creased in a grin. *I haven't had fun like that in years. Thank you, Lord, even if I did take a dunking.*

Flannery sobered. Staring down at her hands, she gave an exclamation.

"I have his keys."

Tag reached for them. "I'll take them to him. He'd be back in short order." He simply gathered all Evan's belongings and walked away.

Everett turned Flannery towards the house, surprised to see Eunice approaching.

"Eunice? I thought that you were gone for the day." Flannery ran to hug her.

"I had intentions of doing just that, but I received a phone call and then an email. We need to talk, child."

Flannery's face paled. "Oh, no. Not him."

"No, it's not about him. It's about your mother. I wasn't satisfied with what you said. I talked to the police chief in your hometown. He hadn't been either. A detective had been looking into the case and found enough evidence that they have opened her death back up."

"They have?" Flannery paled even more. "Not suicide?"

"No, not suicide. They think murder. The new medical examiner is going back over everything. It's been that long that they don't know if they would find any evidence if they exhumed her body. That's still a possibility."

Flannery shuddered. "Who?"

"That's something else we need to speak about. The man who tried to abduct you? They think it's his handiwork."

"I don't understand." Flannery's hands reached for the bread and the sandwich fixings, intent on preparing their lunch.

"Somehow, they think he was involved in her death. They are looking at your father's as well. Something just hadn't set right with that either."

"Dad was an alcoholic. I know that. Did he not just drive off the road?" Flannery looked up as she heard a muffled sound and saw Evan and Tag standing in front of her. "Evan?"

"That's what we wondered too, Flannery. Tag and I were speaking about it last night."

"I see." Flannery's hands stopped moving and Eunice shifted her aside so that she could take over. "That changes everything that I believed about myself."

"It does and it doesn't. For now, it's all just supposition. If it is true, it doesn't change who you are. You are you, a wonderful talented beautiful young lady." Everett reached to hug her. "One who we love and care about deeply. Now, let's eat and then we'll dig into Scripture, to find those verses that you need."

Chapter 12

A week later, Flannery found the Muskoka chair that she preferred, just before the dock started. She flopped down in it, her water bottle hitting the ground. Sam, her almost constant companion, dropped down at her feet, or rather on her feet, she thought. She reached to rub at his head, finding the spot on his neck that he enjoyed rubbed. She smiled as she heard the deep sigh of contentment rise from him.

Her eyes then rose to the lake, seeing the light fog that was rising. It's going to be a hot day, Flannery thought. I can feel it already. She listened to the music of the morning as the birds and the animals roused. Smiling, she watched the chipmunks scurry around, already busy gathering their food.

Flannery thought back over the last few days. She had become a welcome part of Everett and Eunice's family and had even spoken with their daughter. She was anxious to meet her in person, but that wouldn't happen, not likely. Flannery considered the danger that she was in and sighed. She was no further ahead, she thought, in finding out who it was that was after her or why. Did it really have to do with her mother?

She jumped as a mug was set down on the arm of her chair and her eyes flew upwards. Evan was there and dropped down onto the ground beside her. He had become a constant in her life, something that she didn't think she had ever had.

"Good morning, sweetheart. Everett said you were down here."

"Good morning to you. too." She watched him closely. "Don't you have to find something to do for work?"

Evan shrugged. "I have feelers out in the area. I'm just not sure what I want to do."

"Everett asked me the other day what my dreams were. What are yours?" Flannery asked this in an idle manner, not really expecting him to answer.

"They've changed over time, Flannery. As I imagine yours have." He caught the faint snort that she gave. "For me? My dream was always to be a police

---

officer. I was chewed up badly and spit out in my last assignment. We were tracking kidnappers. Only the little boy didn't come home. He had a medical condition that the kidnappers ignored." He felt her hand resting on his head in sympathy. "That took the dream from me. I can join the small force here if I wish. I have been asked to teach my techniques, but I am not a teacher. I am at loose ends for the present."

"Have you considered working with youth?" Flannery was throwing out suggestions, she knew.

Evan nodded. "That's what Dad did. He had a foundation that is still going, helping boys in need. There is a camp not too far from here that he started for all youths, in memory of Mom." A sad look crossed his face. "He missed her that much. He did his best for me, to try and keep me on the straight and narrow as he put it. And to help me discover my dreams." He looked up at her. "What about you?"

"Everett asked me that. I told him my dreams were gone. That I had lost hope." She stared out across the lake, a thoughtful look on her face. "At one time, I had wanted to help young children, to help them achieve their potential. But you need schooling for that. I couldn't afford to go to school, and I was constantly on the move."

"How long did you stay in one place?" Evan and Tag had talked about that before Tag left, trying to get a sense of how the drug dealer had tracked her.

Flannery shrugged. "Maybe six months at the most. I just didn't fit in. I was always the girl from the wrong side of town. The alcoholic's daughter. The drug addict's daughter. Mom didn't start to use until I was around ten, I think. That's about the point where Dad's alcohol abuse had worsened and just before he was killed." She looked down at him. "You're not running screaming from me like everyone else."

"No, I wouldn't do that." Evan's hand found hers and she nestled hers into his strong grasp. "You deserve to be treated as an individual. A beautiful loving lady with a huge heart."

Flannery simply shook her head. "About that man. What else have you learned, and Eunice learned?"

"That you were very fortunate to escape him." Evan's face grew grim. "I had heard rumours of someone like him when I was undercover. A friend who worked the

—

84

streets has been in touch. He warned me to keep an eye on you. That man will be out for revenge now that you have escaped him.”

“I didn’t expect anything else.” She watched as Evan pulled out his phone, frustration in his manner.

“I’m sorry, Flannery. I really need to take this call.” Evan was on his feet, moving away, Sam beside him, sensing Evan’s mood.

Flannery sat for a while, lost in thought before she felt a presence beside her. Looking up, she drew back in fear. She recognized one of the men from when Evan had been beaten. She scrambled from her chair, backing away from him.

“You can’t escape, little lady.” The man leered at her. “The boss wants you to come with me.” He approached her, a hand held out to grasp her arm.

Flannery struggled to escape, fear driving her to scratch at his face. She heard the curses as her fingers found his eyes and his grasp loosened. Fear led speed to her feet, and she fled, not towards the cabin where she would be safe but away from it, towards the forest. Desperation led her to plunge into the shrubbery, finding an

—

animal path that she followed, her head turning every once in a while to listen.

Tripping over an exposed root, Flannery hit the ground, her breath knocked out of her. Her head hit another exposed root and she lay still, blood trickling slowly from the cut that was left. The critters that she had disturbed gradually came back out, sniffing around the large object that lay in their way. They moved around it, giving it glances as they did so before they just went on their way and through their day. The birds once more began their singing as did the insects. She didn't feel the flutter of the butterflies as they landed on her. She didn't hear or feel anything.

Chapter 13

Arriving back at Everett's late that afternoon, Evan entered their mudroom, kicking off his wet sneakers and hanging up his damp jacket. The rain that had threatened had arrived for most of the day and had changed to a drizzle. He rubbed at his hair before he entered the kitchen, greeting the older couple before he looked around.

"Where's Flannery?" He was puzzled. He had left her near the dock when he had to leave.

Eunice spun, shock on her face and looked past him.

"She's not with you? When you disappeared earlier, we thought that she had gone with you."

Everett's face grew grim. "Sam's been upset all day. Every time I had him out, he wanted to head for the dock area."

—

87

Evan's face paled as he heard what they weren't saying. Flannery was not in the cabin and no one had any idea where she was.

"No, I had to leave to meet with someone. I left her near the dock. Sam came with me and I sent him home as I was leaving." Evan pulled on his jacket and shoved his feet into his sneakers, heading out and towards the dock, Sam running ahead of him. "Wait, Sam. Let me catch up."

Evan's hand rested on the dog's head as he heard the growls coming from Sam.

"Where is she, boy? You're not happy. Can you find her even after all this rain?"

Sam looked up at him and gave a bark and then began circling, trying his best to find the lady that he adored almost as much as he did Eunice and Everett. He turned towards the forest and then with a bark, was running that way, Evan following as quickly as he could.

Evan's calls for Sam to slow down and wait for him went unheeded by the dog. He could hear the sounds of his running and his faint yips. When they stopped abruptly, Evan's heart clenched. What had

—

happened? He ran even faster, slipping and sliding on the mud and the grass and the fallen debris, tripping and falling before he picked himself back up and continued.

Sliding to a halt as he found Sam, he frowned. Why had the dog stopped here? He approached Sam, finding the dog on his belly trying his best to rouse Flannery. His nose nudged under her arm so that he could lick at her face. Only he couldn't rouse her. Sam just couldn't understand why his beloved friend was just lying there, not responding to him.

Evan gave a cry and was on his knees beside Sam, pushing the dog away, his hands reaching for Flannery. He turned her over, cradling her in his arms, dismayed at the blood on her face that the drizzle began to wash away. She didn't respond to him either, not to the heartbroken cries that he gave.

Everett approached, having followed Sam and Evan, knowing that if Flannery was around, Sam would find her.

"Here, Evan. Let me take a look." Everett crouched down, his hands moving over Flannery. "She's knocked herself out. Let's get her wrapped into this blanket." He pulled out an emergency blanket and helped Evan wrap her tight, holding her until Evan was on his feet reaching for Flannery.

Evan walked as quickly as he could back towards the cabin, cradling the lady that he now knew he loved more than anything else. Everett walked behind him, his eyes on Flannery as her head bounced against Evan no matter how carefully he was walking. *Lord, he prayed, heal our friend. Don't let her be injured too badly. I can do what I can, but if she needs more help, then we'll have to head into the hospital. I don't know that Evan could handle that. Not being her next of kin. As far as we know, she has no one.*

Eunice took one look at Evan and pointed towards the room that Flannery had claimed.

"In there, Evan. Here. Let me spread out a sheet. Then you get into dry clothes, the pair of you. No, Sam, you can't come in. You need to dry off. And you're muddy." Eunice closed the door behind her, shutting out the men who were so worried about Flannery. Moving quickly, she worked to get Flannery dry and into clean clothes, a towel under her head to soak up the wet from her hair. She turned at last to the door, opening it for Everett.

"She hasn't roused, Everett. She's chilled through and through."

"She had some shelter, but the rain was cold. Evan's working on filling hot water bottles. I threw a blanket into the dryer." He handed it to his wife. "Let me take a look and see what we need to do for her."

Chapter 14

Evan paced outside the closed door, the hot water bottles that he had filled clasped in his arms. They did not warm him, however, his fear was that great for Flannery. Sam sat in front of the door, his head tilted as he listened.

Everett finally opened the door, his hand reaching for the hot water bottles before he nodded to Evan. Sam had slipped past him and stood, his chin on the bed, his eyes on Flannery.

"Everett?" Evan was almost afraid to ask.

"She's still unconscious. And cold. These will help." Everett helped Eunice tuck the bottles around her. "We need to raise her temperature but not too quickly."

Evan nodded, his eyes on Flannery. He approached the bed before he dropped to his knees, his hand reaching to touch her cheek. Her head turned into his touch as she gave a soft sigh.

"Flannery? Can you hear me?" Evan's voice was low and hopeful that she could.

Eunice watched before she finally moved to touch his shoulder.

"Come, Evan. You need to get something hot into you. You can come back." Eunice watched as he reluctantly left, his head turning at the doorway so that he could study the younger woman.

It was after midnight when Flannery finally stirred, burrowing down under the blankets. She was warm, she thought, her eyes flickering open as Eunice spoke with her.

"Flannery? Can you talk with me?"

"Eunice? It's dark. I need to sleep."

"I know you do." Eunice's voice had a tinge of humour. "But we need to check you out. You fell yesterday and knocked yourself out."

"I did? I don't remember." She squinted at Eunice before with a soft sigh she slept.

Evan was at the doorway, watching, as Eunice finally turned. Her hand drew him away as she partially closed the bedroom door.

"She was awake for a bit, Evan. She's sleeping now."

"Sleeping? That's good?" Evan was confused, not remembering the first aid that he had studied, his concern for Flannery that great.

"It is. It's a natural sleep. Off to bed with you, now. She'll need you in the morning." Eunice watched with compassion as Evan reluctantly walked away, her heart raised in prayer for the younger couple. Both she and Everett could see them falling in love with one another, but so unsure of their feelings that they wouldn't speak of them.

Evan didn't sleep. Instead, he sat by the window in the room he was using, his eyes on the night, his prayers raising for Flannery. He was puzzled as to what had happened. The rain had washed away any evidence of why she had run. And he wasn't even sure that she would remember. That happened sometimes with a concussion. The person didn't remember what had happened just before they were hurt.

He rose with the early dawn of a new day, heading for the kitchen to make the coffee and put on the kettle for Eunice. With his own mug of coffee in his hand, he walked towards the dock, Sam pacing beside him. He frowned as Sam's hackles rose near the chair that Flannery favoured.

"What's up, boy?" Evan stopped, staring around before he saw Sam nosing an object in the mud. He reached for it and then froze. A syringe. That had not been there yesterday morning. And he knew that it was not Flannery's.

"What did you find, Evan?" Everett spoke from beside him.

"That. A syringe. Sam alerted to it. It wasn't there yesterday."

Everett stared at the syringe that Evan had picked up with the plastic bag he pulled from his pocket.

"That could be why she ran. Eunice said that Flannery's still asleep. She was awake a couple of more times in the night. Flannery told her that she has a horrible headache."

"No doubt." Evan stared at the syringe. "I'll have to take this in and have it tested. I suspect it will hold drugs of some kind."

"More than likely." Everett pointed back at the house. "Breakfast is waiting, Evan. Let's eat and then you can head into town with that."

Eunice stared at the syringe before she stared at Evan.

"You found it where?"

"By Flannery's chair. Sam found it."

"That's why she ran. Someone was here. You know, Sam was upset all day, trying to head for the woods and we kept calling him back." Eunice rubbed at her face. "If we had let him, maybe we would have found Flannery sooner."

"But you didn't know that she was here." Evan looked around as he heard footsteps and then was across the room, his arms sweeping Flannery into a hug. "You're up."

"I am. My head hurts, Evan." Flannery's eyes were barely open, the light hurt them that much.

"We know, sweetheart. You have a concussion. Everett wants to take you to the

---

clinic in town, have the doctor look you over."

Flannery shrugged. "I suppose. Is there any juice?"

"Sit here, child." Eunice pointed to a chair. "We have juice. I wouldn't suggest much more than that for you this morning."

Flannery shook her head and then groaned. "Now, why'd I do that? Between the headache, the dizziness and nausea, I don't think I'll go anywhere."

Chapter 15

Two days later, Flannery sat on the couch near the fireplace, her legs curled up under her. She had wrapped herself in a blanket, still feeling chilled. She refused to look at Evan, who sat perched in Everett's rocking chair, his eyes on her.

"Flannery? We need to talk."

"Not today." Flannery was frustrated at being sick and hurt, and she refused to let Evan heal her.

"We do. I found a syringe where you had been seated. It contained a sedative."

Flannery shrugged. "I don't remember." She finally looked up at Evan, her eyes shuttered. She saw the concern for her on his face as well as another emotion that she just refused to understand. "Go away, Evan."

"No, I won't." Evan was adamant that he would not.

"Go away. You're hovering. I don't like that." It was not true, her words, but she was trying to avoid Evan getting hurt again. She figured that as long as he was near her, that danger still existed.

Evan sat back, shock on his face. His mouth opened and closed before he stood, his eyes on her. Hurt stood on his face, the hurt of a little boy who had been told he couldn't play with his friend's toys.

"Go away, Evan. I don't like it when you hover over me." Flannery refused to look up.

Finally turning, Evan walked away, past Eunice who stood in the archway to the kitchen, a hand to her mouth at Flannery's words. Everett watched from where he stood near the woodpile, a hand on Sam's head to keep him beside him.

"He's hurting, Sammy boy. And we can't help him. Not this time." Everett stared after Evan and then down at Sam. "Ok, Sammy. Off you go. Go with Evan. He needs a friend with him."

Sam looked up at his master, gave a low woof and then ran after Evan. He nudged at Evan's hand as the man sat on his front porch steps, sorrow on his face. Evan reached to hug Sam, unable to speak, the tears he was fighting too near the surface. His heart raised in prayer, he couldn't even form the words but he knew that the Holy Spirit would pray for him.

Everett dropped an armful of logs into the wood box in the kitchen before he too stood watching Flannery.

"What happened, love?" He kept his voice low.

"She sent him away, Everett. Told him to stop hovering. That she didn't like it." Eunice leaned her head against Everett. "He's hurting, love."

"He is. Sam's with him. Not much comfort, I know, but he's not on his own." Everett finally turned and motioned Eunice to come with him to the back porch. "How is she?"

"Doc said that she'd have headaches for a while. The dizziness concerned him. If it continues, then he'll treat it. The nausea Flannery says has gone. What do we do?"

"Not much we can do, love. Except for pray. And watch." Everett stared out across the lake. "Evan got the report back already on the syringe. It contained a sedative."

"A sedative?" Eunice nodded. "Of course. Sedate her, take her away and then play with her mind. If they kept her sedated to a certain degree, that would work."

"It would. It worries me that they would come right onto our property to try and take her."

"I know. We can't fence it off. James is coming out with more motion sensor lights and cameras for us. He feels they are needed for now. He'll remove them when this is all over. If it ever is."

"It will be." Everett turned as he heard the door open. "Flannery? What would you like to do?"

Flannery shrugged, her eyes haunted. "Eunice, have you heard anything more about my Mom?"

"No, not since we spoke. The chief said it would take a bit to investigate. He has promised to call me or you as soon as he has any word."

"But I don't have a phone." Flannery drew in a shaky breath. "I never had the money for one."

"There's one on the table for you. We added it to our plan." Everett held up a hand. "It's what we would do for our own daughter, Flannery. Do you think we would do any less for you? You've become part of our family, a part that we don't want to lose."

"Thank you." Flannery's voice was barely audible. She looked around. "Where's Evan?"

"You sent him home, Flannery, and he went. You need to talk with him." Eunice's arm around her shoulders turned Flannery back into the house. "You two really do need to talk."

"I know. I'm just not used to people watching out for me or hovering over me. I haven't had that for so long." Flannery's voice was matter of fact, with no emotion in it at all.

"I know, love. But you do now. Here, have a seat. We need to talk as well." Eunice watched her friend. "I know you're hurting, Flannery, and scared. I have seen it too often to beat around the bush with you. Let's make some plans for the next few weeks."

Flannery searched Eunice's face, seeing trust in her and love for her young friend.

"I should leave, Eunice. If they tried to take me like you said, they may hurt you or Everett."

"We've faced our share of danger, love. I did as an officer. I faced death on more than one occasion. I have seen things I wouldn't want anyone else to see." She paused, choosing her next words carefully. "Evan is the same, only it is worse for him. He was on the streets or undercover. That means he saw things that will haunt him forever. He is starting to heal, partly because of you." Eunice reached for Flannery's hand. "I can see that he is falling in love with you. Don't shove him away. Listen to his words. Listen to his heart. He won't say it in words. And listen to your heart. More importantly, pray about it and listen to what God is telling you."

Chapter 16

Raising his head the next morning, Evan finally rose from his desk and walked to the door, pulling it open. He frowned. He knew that he had heard a noise. He cautiously walked across the porch, searching for what he had heard. His eyes softened as he saw Flannery standing on the walk, her eyes on him, not willing to come any closer to him.

"Flannery? You're here." Evan reached to draw the door closed behind him. "What can I do for you?"

"Can we talk, Evan? I need to apologize for yesterday. I didn't mean to hurt you."

Evan heard the contrite tone that she was using and saw the sadness in her eyes. He simply reached to pull her into a hug, her face buried against him as she began to weep. Sam stood up at her, trying to reach her face to give her kisses.

Finally, Evan just swept her into his arms and turned back to sit on the porch steps, Flannery cuddled close to him. Sam sat on her other side, a paw on her leg.

"Flannery? Can you stop crying?" Evan was out of his element, he thought.

She finally nodded. "I'm sorry. I didn't mean to do that."

Evan simply smiled, his thumb out to wipe away the tears.

"You're forgiven. Please, don't send me away again."

"I won't." She looked up at him, seeing what Eunice had seen. His feelings for her were out in the open. "But we need to talk. Eunice had word this morning that Mom's death was an overdose, but she didn't take it herself, they don't think. At least, not willingly. She had left some paperwork that no one had ever looked at. She named people that were drug runners and dealers."

"Did she? So, we're looking at murder. Tag and I talked about that the last night that he was up here."

"Did you? It changes things."

"It does, sort of. But you are still you." Evan's arm tightened around her. "Have you remembered anything about that day?"

Flannery shook her head. "I try but I just get so scared that my mind stays blank. That syringe?"

"The syringe? The one I took in? It had a sedative in it."

Flannery paled. "It did? So, I wouldn't have known what happened to me?"

"No, not at first. We suspect that they would have kept you lightly sedated and possibly introduced you to other drugs, making you so desperate to get them that you'd sell your soul to do just that. That's how they work. You would have been out there delivering packages, just to get your next fix. And you would have been the one going to jail. They would cover their tracks and do that well."

Flannery paled even further and shook in her fear. Sam whined, his tongue reached to lick at her face. She wrapped an arm around him.

"Evan? How do we do this? How do we find him? He's done this to others."

"He has. We have a name for him." Evan gave the name, watching her face closely.

"I don't know him. I don't remember ever seeing him." Flannery frowned.

"You may not have. Eunice has talked to you?"

"She has. Not that it helped any." Evan smiled at the tone in her voice. "She was asking questions that I can't answer."

"I'll help with the answers if you like." He bit back his grin as she frowned at him. "I can, you know."

"I know. It's what she's asking that I don't know how to answer."

"If it's about you and me, then I would say we date."

"Evan!" Her plaintive wail sounded through the woods. "How can you say that?"

"Because it's true. It's what I would like to do. Of course, out here, we don't have many places to go."

"No." Flannery moved away from him, to walk around the cabin. She appeared back in front of him, Sam keeping pace with her. "How do we do this? I'm too dangerous to know."

"No, not really." Evan leaned back on his hands, his legs stretched out down the steps.

"I am, Evan. Look what happened to you the day after we met." Flannery was more worried about Evan than she wanted to admit.

"I shouldn't have gone out. Not on my own."

"But they would have still broken in. And you wouldn't have had time to warn me."

"I would have." Evan was on his feet, his hand reaching for hers. "Dad put in something else that I had fun with." He led her to the kitchen, to a seemingly innocent wall. "Here. See this knot in the trim? Push it."

She stared at him, not sure what he meant.

"Push it, sweetheart." When she didn't, he reached to lightly push at it.

Flannery's mouth flew open as she gaped at first the opening and then at Evan.

"It's a tunnel. Dad doesn't know who put it in. We think someone used it for smuggling years ago. It leads down to the lake. We have always kept a canoe there. Sometimes, Dad would wake me up in the middle of the time, pretending that we were under attack and had to flee. He made it an adventure."

"Your father sounds wonderful. You have such memories with him." Flannery stepped forward, looking around. "Is there a light?"

"No. I keep a flashlight here on this hook. Come on. We can go down if you like. That way, you'll have a sense of what it's like. I think you'll have an opportunity to use it at some point. Lead the way, Sam."

Chapter 17

Flannery turned the next morning as she heard footsteps approaching her. She and Eunice had ventured to town, Eunice stating that Flannery needed to get out of the cabin. She knew that she certainly did. She frowned at the woman who stood in front of her.

"Hi. You're a friend of Eunice's?" The woman, around her own age, waited for Flannery to speak.

Flannery was not sure how to respond. She didn't want to acknowledge that and put Eunice in trouble. Eunice appeared at that point.

"Suzy! How wonderful to see you! You're back for the summer?" Eunice reached to hug the younger woman.

"Just for the last couple of months of it, I suspect. Dad and Mom are selling their home and sent me up here to see what needed to be done to get their cottage ready to live in full time. Not that there is much to do." She laughed, her green eyes lighting up with her humour.

"That's good. Have you met Flannery?" Eunice's arm was around Flannery. "She's a friend of ours. In fact, she's living with us while we struggle through my book."

Flannery was cautious as Suzy greeted her. She frowned. There was just something off about her, she decided. Her life had led her to be cautious around others. She didn't want Eunice to be offended but really didn't want to go to lunch as Eunice had suggested.

Eunice watched Flannery carefully, sensing that she was uncomfortable. She sighed to herself. Yes, Suzy was pushy, but she had always been like that. She listened closely to the questions that Suzy was asked and frowned.

Flannery finally looked at Eunice, a plea in her eyes.

"Suzy, this was nice, but Flannery and I need to run. We're at a point in my book that we need to do some research and that has to be done this afternoon." Eunice was on her feet, paying for the meal, ushering the two younger women out. She didn't respond when Suzy asked if she could come to visit.

"Can I, Eunice?"

Eunice stared at her for a moment before she shook her head.

"We're deep into the book right now, Suzy. I'm not sure when would be a good time but right now it's not."

Suzy pouted, sure that Evan would be around if there was another young woman there. She had her sights set on him and would be willing to take out anyone that she saw as competition.

Flannery breathed a sigh of relief. She turned her head as she felt eyes watching her. The man who had accosted her at Eunice's stood nearby, his eyes flickering between Suzy and herself. It suddenly crystallized in her mind. Suzy was a plant. She was trying to get Flannery off on her own.

Linking her arm with Eunice, Flannery gave a smile that didn't reach her eyes.

"Eunice is correct. We do have research to do, and we must be at it. It was nice to meet you." Flannery gave a smile of dismissal as she walked off with Eunice, leaving Suzy angry behind her.

"Didn't work?" The man approached Suzy.

"No, it didn't. She'll not be willing to go out with me to lunch on her own. She suspected something."

"You were too forceful and inquisitive. He told you that." The man's hand pulled her with him to his vehicle and shoved her inside before he slipped behind the wheel. "He won't be pleased with you."

"I know." Suzy glared at him. "Take me home. And I don't mean here. I mean back to the city. Dad and Mom are on their own."

"Tsk. Tsk. Such a way to leave your parents." His sarcasm made her even angrier.

"Just shut up.

Chapter 18

Evan slipped to a seating position beside Flannery as she sat in her favourite chair. She turned her head to watch him, a frown on her face. Evan had stood for the longest time just watching her and had finally moved to take his seat.

"Evan?"

"Flannery? How are you tonight?" Evan wanted to ask a question but wasn't sure just how to do that.

"I'm okay. At least, I was." She bit at her lip. "What do you know about Suzy?"

"Who? Suzy? Oh, her." Evan was discomforted. Suzy had kept trying to get his attention, but his senses had warned him about her. He had always kept his distance. "Not a lot. Her parents have a cottage up here. Why?"

"Because she had lunch with Eunice and me. She was asking questions that seemed innocent until you really listened.

She was prying, Evan, trying to find out information about me that she didn't need to know."

"I see. What else happened?" His hand reached for her, his clasp welcomed.

"I saw that man from that day. I remembered him." Flannery turned to Evan, fear suddenly on her face. "I remember. He tried to get me to go with him and I fought him, running when I could. He seemed awfully interested in what Suzy was saying. I don't think it was idle curiosity. I think he knew her."

"He did? We'll look into that. I'll send the names onto Tag. He's still working on it when he can."

"He is? He shouldn't be."

"No, he should. You were assaulted in his patrol area. He'll work on it to solve it. And I have no doubt that he will." Evan's thumb rubbed along her hand. "We're trying, sweetheart."

"I know. It's just so frustrating. I am worried that Eunice and Everett will be hurt because of me."

"They are aware of the risks." Evan grew silent, content just to sit with

Flannery. "How about we go out for dinner one night?"

Her head shot around, and she stared at him. "What did you just ask?"

"I asked you out on a date." Evan grinned at her. "Game to go out with me?"

Flannery shook her head. "You know I'm dangerous to know."

"I know, sweetheart. And it doesn't make a whit of difference. I want to take you out for a meal. It's not going to be fancy. The only restaurant open late is the fish and chip shop."

"Well, I was expecting you to be in a tux and all. A real fancy restaurant." She kept her smile hidden, stalling, watching as he shifted in his seat, growing worried that she would refuse him. "When were you thinking?"

"Tomorrow night?" Evan was hopeful.

"I see. How be I let you know the day after tomorrow whether I will or not? Does that work?" Flannery hid her face, unable to keep the smile away from it.

"Sure. That works." Evan's head suddenly shot around as he stared at her, his eyes narrowing. "What do you mean? The day after tomorrow?"

"Just what I said." Flannery began to laugh, her musical laugh filling the air. "Got you."

Evan realized that he had been had and began to laugh as well. Neither saw the man hovering at the edge of the woods, listening to their conversation. He grew angry, listening to the laughter. He was under pressure to bring Flannery to his boss. Only she was never alone. She was with someone or the dog. And he feared dogs more than his boss.

Flannery looked up at that point and shivered.

"Someone is out here, Evan."

"I know. How be we head in? I don't like you out here at dusk." He pulled her to her feet and walked back to the cabin without dropping her hand.

Flannery watched that evening as her three companions worked away on her mystery, as they called it. The police chief from her hometown had been in touch. He had confirmed with her that her mother's death was an overdose. Plain and simple overdose. He had had the medical examiner go back over everything. He apologized for the wrong reason for death being given.

When she asked about her father, he had been silent before he spoke. Yes, her father was intoxicated that night. But going back over the photos, the detective had found what he thought was evidence that her father had been run off the road. There was paint on the car that shouldn't have been there. He was unsure though if they could ever track down who had been there.

Flannery had thanked him, thoughtfully handing Eunice back her phone. She had turned back to her work, not seeing the glances Eunice kept throwing her. Eunice had sighed, knowing that she had to let it lie, to let Flannery talk with her. But if she hadn't by the next day, she would talk with Flannery.

Chapter 19

Eunice finally rose late the next afternoon, stretching and then rubbing at the small of her back. They had been hard at work since the quick lunch they had taken. She studied Flannery, a small smile on her face. *She's avoiding me, isn't she, Lord? I pray for her safety and for resolution of this, whatever it is, and quickly. Evan is moving in on her, spending time with her. I don't know that he will wait until it's resolved, and Flannery will not want to put him at risk. We're torn here, Lord, and could use some answers.*

"Flannery? Enough for the day. We'll be needing to get to our meal."

Flannery glanced up and at the clock and gave a small sound.

"Evan will be here shortly, won't he?"

"I would suspect so if he isn't all ready. I thought I heard his car." Eunice turned back at that point, startled at the uncertainty on Flannery's face. "Flannery?"

"He asked me to go out with him for a meal tonight. I shouldn't have said yes." Flannery wrapped her arms around herself even as she stared at the computer monitor.

"He would have weighed the risks before he asked, Flannery." Eunice pulled over a chair to sit beside the younger woman and then began to pray for her, covering her with the promises of God's protection.

Flannery looked up in surprise when Eunice finished.

"Thank you. No one has ever done that for me."

"No? We have been in our own prayers. We will continue to do that with you, Flannery. We have been remiss." Eunice hugged her and then sat back. "So, how fancy?"

Giggling, Flannery admitted that she had teased Evan the night before. Eunice began to laugh, stating that it served him right.

"The fish and chip shop, is it?" At Flannery's nod, Eunice thought for a moment. "Jeans and a nice top. Do you have one?"

Shaking her head, Flannery admitted that she didn't. Eunice was on her feet, pulling Flannery with her.

"Here. I had bought this with thoughts of giving it to Lydia. She would say to let you have it." She held up a beautiful jade sweater, lightweight, just perfect for the temperature that day.

"I can't take it." Flannery's eyes were soft as she studied the sweater and felt it even as she protested.

"Take it and wear it, love." Eunice looked around. "Now, scurry off and get dressed. I hear Evan's voice."

A short while later, Evan seated Flannery at a table in the restaurant, not catching the speculative glances shot his way. He had never brought a date there. In fact, the residents weren't even sure that he dated.

Flannery looked around, uncomfortable at first, but relaxing at Evan's teasing and his comments on the patrons.

"You need to stop, Evan. I won't be able to eat." Flannery's face was flushed with laughter, making her seem even more beautiful to Evan.

Unrepentant, he just grinned and continued to eat. He frowned as he looked up, ready to say something.

"Flannery?" When she didn't respond, his hand reached for hers, covering it. "Flannery, what happened? I've lost you."

"You have. That man is here. Seated behind you. Can't we go anywhere without him following us?"

"Is he?" Evan kept his tone even. "Eat up, sweetheart. Then, I'll take you through the kitchen to meet the owners. They are a wonderful older couple. They've been here for years. In fact, they're wanting to retire and are looking for someone to take over."

"Why don't you?" Flannery asked the question that he had never thought about.

"You know, I never thought about that. I'll pray over it, that's for sure." He rose, his hand out for hers, not seeing the smiles sent their way. Evan was well-liked in the community, willing to help anyone who had a need.

Evan led her finally from the back door around to his SUV, his eyes searching, senses alert. He closed the door after her, his hand resting against it for a moment before he turned. Only he never made it all the way around. Running footsteps alerted him almost too late that someone was coming. His body slammed into the vehicle and then dropped to the ground from the blows that he took.

Flannery screamed and then her hand fumbled to find the lock on the door. She cringed back as the man hammered at the window and yanked at the door handle, all to no avail. Her arms covered her head as she crouched down, praying for someone to come.

Her prayers were answered. The officer on duty that night had just pulled into the restaurant parking lot, intent on his dinner, when he spied the commotion and throwing open his door, was across the pavement, the man's wrists handcuffed behind him.

Dooley dropped to his knees beside Evan, carefully helping him to sit up.

"Evan? What is this all about?"

"Arrest him, please, Dooley. Not just for this. He tried to abduct Flannery a few days ago."

"And who is Flannery?" Dooley was puzzled, not seeing anyone else.

"Help me up." Once on his feet, Evan reached for his key fob, unlocking the door and pulling it open. He simply reached for Flannery, finding that she fought him until she recognized his voice. Then her arms were around his neck as she hid her face against him.

"Evan? What is going on?"

"This is Flannery. It's a long story, but someone tried to abduct her a few weeks ago. I happened on it and brought her to Everett and Eunice. She has no family. Since then, they have tried at least twice to abduct her. I had a bad beating just after we arrived."

"I heard about that. Just didn't know why."

The men spoke for a few more moments before Dooley took his prisoner and headed off. He looked with longing at the restaurant and shook his head. *Not tonight,* he thought. *Another night with a stale sandwich.*

Flannery watched him walk away.

"He was here for his meal, wasn't he?"

"More than likely. It's where they come at night." Evan stated at her before his face lit up. "Come on. We'll order a meal for him. They'll deliver it to him."

Chapter 20

Early the next morning, Evan padded across the living room in his cabin, his bare feet hitting softly on the wide pine planks. His mug hit the desk as he dropped into his black leather desk chair, a gift from his father. He reached to pull up his email, nodding as he saw one from Tag. *Thank you, Lord. Maybe now we can get some answers.*

Evan sat back eventually, having read and re-read the email and the attachments. *Tag*, he thought, *the drive and curiosity that brought your family from Scotland are alive and well in you. No doubt about it. Dad would have said you were going at this like a dog worrying a bone.*

He looked up, his eyes narrowing. Dooley had called him late the night before and informed him that the man was wanted in numerous municipalities. It was unlikely that he would be free again to bother them. But he had refused to talk, to tell them who he worked for. Did Evan have any idea?

There had been silence on the other end of the phone when Evan had spoken a name.

"Him?" Dooley's voice held incredulity.

"Him. He's the one who was after Flannery. I saved her that day. He's been after her since. We think to become a mule."

"A mule? He's a known drug lord. No one has been able to catch him though."

"I suspect that will be me and Flannery. Pray for us, Dooley. She's in a lot of danger. She'll walk away if she thinks that will protect either myself or Everett and Eunice."

"I see. I thought that last night." Evan heard papers rustling. "Listen, I need you to come in tomorrow and make your statement. Flannery, too."

"We'll be there." Evan had set his phone aside after he had promised that, reaching for his Bible instead. He needed the comfort that only his communion with God would bring.

He sat back eventually from the community directory he had been scanning, his eyes on one particular name. *He's prominent in this community, Lord. How do we do this? No one will believe us.* Evan sighed, knowing that he would need to brush off his street cop skills and figure out a way. And that meant likely involving Flannery and maybe even Eunice and Everett.

Eunice nodded as Evan quickly spoke to her later that morning. He had appeared just after they had cleaned up from their breakfast.

"I've suspected him for years, Evan. So this is not new. There have been multiple reports of strange vehicles, both car and boat, at his place. Even the odd floatplane landing. We have had to just watch and monitor him." Eunice shared a look with Everett. "This is going to get worse for you two, you do realize that?"

"I do. Did Flannery say anything about last night?"

Eunice shook her head. "No. When I asked her, she said the meal and company were enjoyable. It was the after-effects that she could have done without. She walked away without saying another word." Her gaze turned towards her office. "What happened?"

"The man who tried to abduct her happened. I didn't see him in time and he took me down. Flannery had the sense to lock the doors of the SUV. She was inside already. Dooley happened to come in for his dinner and arrested him."

"I see. Do you have a name?" Everett leaned against the counter, stirring his mug of coffee.

"I do. Jason Bird."

"Jason Bird? Oh, I know that name." Eunice's mind drifted back. "Yes, he's been wanted for so many incidents. No one had been able to arrest him. Until now. He'll not be out soon. Knowing who he works for? He'll be on his own, with no money for bail."

"That's what Dooley and I figure. Listen, Flannery and I need to head for town to give our statements. Can you spare her for a couple of hours?"

"I can. She's up to date on what I have done so far. She's been doing some research for me. She's good at that."

"She is? Wonderful. You'll put her skills to good use." Evan walked away at that point, leaving the older couple staring after him.

"He's going to put himself out there. You do know that." Everett shook his head.

"He will. He will polish off his undercover and street cop skills and do just that. I worry for him, Everett." Eunice walked into her husband's hug. "They're falling in love. If Flannery thinks that he is at risk, she'll walk away from him."

"I know that she will. We'll have to bathe them in prayer. The next few weeks will be difficult." Everett reached to pour himself another mug of coffee. "When does Lydia get home?"

Eunice squinted at the calendar, her reading glasses on the desk in the office.

"Next week, I think she said. Wednesday?"

"That's good. I'll be glad to have her home." Everett walked away, intent on finding something constructive to do, Sam pacing beside him. "Well, Sammy, what shall we do today? Think the fish are biting? Want to go fishing?" He was rewarded with a low woof.

Evan reached for the pen that Flannery was tapping on the desk. He could tell that she was not really concentrating on her work.

"Evan? You're here?" She looked up, a smile lighting her face before she frowned. "How are you today?"

"I'm sore but I've been worse. Listen. Dooley called. He needs us to come in and make our statements."

"I knew that. I was going to head in only I had no ride." Flannery stood, surprised that Evan swept her into a hug and prayed for her. She was sure that she felt him kiss the top of her head but decided that she was mistaken.

Dooley watched the couple as they stood speaking with his supervisor and shook his head. Evan has found his lady, I guess, hasn't he, Lord? We always wondered who she would be. Living as she has? She's a perfect match to what he has gone through on the streets.

"Dooley?" Evan had approached. "Thanks."

"No problem, Evan. Just stay out of trouble."

"I'll try but if they come after Flannery, I won't."

"Didn't think you would. Are you up for our Bible study tomorrow night?"

———

"I should be. Is there one at the same time for the ladies?"

"There is. Flannery should come."

"I'll ask her." Evan reached for her hand as she moved to stand beside him. "If she agrees, then you'll see both of us."

"If I agree to what?" Flannery refused to move until Evan sighed.

"There are Bible studies at the church tomorrow night. I go to the men's. There's a ladies' one that you might enjoy."

"I'll think about it. I'm just not sure about putting anyone at risk." Flannery turned to watch him as he drove away from the town.

"I get that. So does everyone else. We'll make sure that you're safe."

"I know that you'll try. Now that he's arrested, how do I know who is out there?"

Evan shot her a look before he nodded. *Lord, she's right. Protect her. Cover her with Your hand. Hide her in the hollow of the rock. Please, dear Lord? I don't want my lady hurt.*

Chapter 21

Early the next morning, Flannery poured her cup of tea and grabbed the Bible that Eunice had insisted on buying for her. Flannery had admitted that she didn't have one and had wanted one until she figured God had given up on her.

"He'll never do that, Flannery. Not for one second. He's there with you, no matter what you have gone through. He loves you that much. He has likely provided protection for you without you even being aware of that." Eunice had enveloped her into a hug as she spoke.

Flannery had nodded. "I guess. I just thought that He would leave me, not want me."

"Oh, love. He wants you very much, enough to send His Son for your salvation. I would suspect that He arranged for Evan to be there at that very time you needed him."

"He would do that?" Flannery had been surprised, watching as Eunice nodded. "I guess I have a poor image of God or a father. Not having had one is difficult. I mean, I went to church and Sunday School. I did take the offer of salvation, but I have slipped away from that."

"Not far enough, Flannery. Not far enough that God can't reach out His hand and draw you back. He does that."

Eunice had watched as Flannery had nodded and then walked away, a thoughtful look on her face. Her prayers followed her young friend.

Sam paced beside his beloved female, his eyes on her face, as she walked towards the dock. Flannery paused, her eyes closing as she drew in a deep breath of fresh crisp air.

"Father, they tell me that You are still there. That You love me more than anyone else. I moved away from You. Help me to find my way back. I fear for my friends, though, Lord. And I don't want them hurt. I will leave if that is what happens. It already has to Evan."

Sam's low growl caught at her attention and she stared down at him. His hackles were raised as he paced towards her chair. Flannery sighed. Someone had been around again. *Now, what this time,* she wondered.

She stared down at the envelope on her chair before she raised her head to look around. Fear stood out on her face. *Someone had been around, once more,* she thought. She reached for the envelope, turning it over and over in her hands. There was no name on it but she had no doubt that it was meant for her.

Evan found her not too long later. A hug and a kiss on her cheek greeted her, causing her to turn to him, surprise on her face, a hand on her cheek to cover the spot.

"Good morning, sweetheart." Evan studied her face, seeing something lurking in her eyes. "And what can we get up to today? It's Saturday. Eunice won't want you working."

"I know. She told me that last night. I would, you know." Flannery had been frustrated when Eunice had laid it on the line for her. No working on Saturday or Sunday, she declared. Flannery had protested to no avail.

"I know you would. So does she." Evan dropped to the ground beside her, his hand reaching to ruffle Sam's ears. "You're troubled."

"I am." She held out the envelope. "This was on my chair this morning. It's not damp so it wasn't there for long."

"A letter? What did it say?" Evan reached for it, his eyes on her.

"I didn't open it. I'm too scared. Evan, this is getting worse. They keep coming after me. I need to leave."

"Not happening. If you leave, I come after you. I told you that already. Now that I've found my lady, I'm not letting her go." Evan had been staring at the envelope, not realizing that he had just laid his heart out for her to accept or reject.

Flannery stared at him. "Evan?" When he looked up, she hesitated, not sure if she should even be asking him the question that she needed to. "Did you mean that?"

"Mean what?" Evan's brow furrowed as he tried to remember what he had just said.

"That I'm your lady?" Flannery was hopeful that he had but didn't think so. She was just too dangerous, she thought.

———

"I did. You are my sweetheart, the lady that I've been waiting for." Evan's hand rested on her cheek. "Now, about this?" He held up the envelope.

"That!" She poked at it. "I didn't open it."

"I see. Waiting for me?" He didn't look at her, instead inspecting the envelope before he pulled out the tucked-in flap and looked inside. "A photo?" He dropped it out, turning it over with the edge of the envelope.

"It's us. Down by the lake." Flannery leaned against him. "That was Thursday afternoon."

"It was. And taken from the lake." He looked up and studied said lake. "I don't remember seeing anyone."

"There were some canoes and a kayak. I think the kayak had stopped. I thought the person was just adjusting his life vest."

"Adjusting it under guise of taking this photo." Evan sighed. "This changes it."

"No, not really. We know that they are watching us, waiting for an opportunity to nab me. This proves it." She tilted her head. "What's on the back of it?"

"I didn't see that." Evan turned it over. "A phone number? That's odd. I'll have Tag run it." He sent off photos of the front and back of what he held and then tucked them into his pocket. "I'll get it to Dooley. Now, what shall we do for the day?"

Flannery stared at him. "What would you suggest?"

"Have you been out in a canoe yet?" When she shook her head, he reached for her hand. "Then, that's what we'll do. I have a lunch packed, hoping that maybe you would consider it. Come on. Sorry, Sam, you have to stay home. I'll bring her back." He raised a hand at Everett who stood on the back deck. "They know we're together."

Flannery simply nodded, her hand in his, glad to be going somewhere where just maybe no one could reach her.

Chapter 22

Monday found Eunice and Flannery in town. Eunice had had to speak with one of the officers that she worked with, Flannery wasn't sure just why. She waited almost impatiently in the foyer of the little building that housed the police. Dooley stood for a moment watching her before he approached.

"Flannery? And how are you?"

Flannery spun at his voice, a hand going to her throat.

"You scared me. I didn't hear you."

"No, you didn't. You were lost in thought. Not a good idea." Dooley grinned at her. "But then you thought you were safe here inside this building." He gestured with his hand.

"I did. I'm waiting for Eunice." She frowned at him. "What have you found out?"

"About?" He grinned again. "Not much. I have been in touch with Evan's friend, Tag. We're working through that paperwork. But you? Evan dropped off that photo yesterday. Not a good thing."

"No, it's not. But it's always what happens, isn't it? Photos. Letters. Packages. Observers. Tails."

Dooley's grin had widened as she spoke. "I see that you have a whole list of things yet to happen. I pray that they never do." He sobered. "Tag is worried about you. The leader has disappeared. We think he's moved to this area, but we can't locate him. You need to be extra cautious."

"I will be, but I still don't get why me."

"That we will ask him when we arrest him. Did you ever have any contact with someone who ran drugs, dropped off parcels that they didn't know the contents of?"

Flannery stared at him, her thoughts running back over the years before she paled.

"No one ever asked me that. I think I did." She swayed in her fright, enough that his hand came out to steady her.

"You did? Can you remember anything about them?" Dooley looked around before he led her to the chairs that sat off to the side. "Talk to me, Flannery. Tell me what you can remember and names if possible."

Flannery nodded, her eyes on Eunice as she approached and then sat beside Flannery, an arm around her.

"Flannery? What is Dooley saying to you?"

"He asked if I knew anyone who ran drugs or whatever. I do." She turned to Eunice. "I told him that no one had asked me that before."

"We were remiss, Flannery. Everett asked me that last night and I was going to speak with you today." She pulled out a pad of paper and a pen, Dooley grinning as he held up his own. "Okay. Let's see what you have to say." She watched as Evan approached, shaking her head slightly at him and stopping him in his tracks. He retreated to wait.

Flannery's eyes closed as she thought back over her life. She began to name people, giving where she knew them from and what they had said to her. Eunice and Dooley exchanged looks, nodding at her memory. She's good, Eunice thought. This may well solve it.

She finally stopped talking, raising her eyes to see Evan watching her, confidence in her on his face.

"I think that's all. Will it help?"

"I would suspect so." Dooley looked back over his list. "You're good. You have an awesome memory. We'll look this over. I'll forward it on to Tag with your permission."

"I'm done then?" At their nod, Flannery was on her feet, almost running to Evan to be caught in a large hug.

"Okay, sweetheart?" His voice was whispered in her ear.

"I am now. You're here." She leaned back. "How did you know?"

"Everett mentioned that you and Eunice were headed this way and he's waiting outside for us. He wants to treat his ladies to lunch." Evan shared a look with Dooley. "That is if you're up to it. And then we'll talk about what was just going on."

"It's okay. I can give you what I told them. Dooley just asked a question and the floodgates of memories opened. Did you say something about lunch? I want to forget this."

"I did." Eunice had approached. "Eunice, Everett is taking you out for lunch. Did you know?"

"No, I didn't but I think it's a wonderful idea. Let's go, you two."

"I don't know, Eunice. Evan might have somewhere else that he needs to be. He's so popular, you know." Flannery winked at Eunice, who choked on her laughter.

Evan hugged Flannery tighter. "The only place I need to be is with you. Let's go, ladies."

Chapter 23

Evan turned from his computer, distress on his face. He had just read an email that Tag had sent to both himself and Eunice. He had confirmed some of the names that Flannery had given. He sighed. It was late at night and too late to go and find her.

He reached for his phone, sending off a text message instead, with an *I love you* and hearts attached. He didn't expect a response but was pleasantly surprised to see one fly back to him in just seconds.

Evan smiled. *Hearts, is it? Does that mean what I think it does? Lord, she's hurting and not sure of anything right now. Please heal my lady. Let the dreams that she has set aside come to fruition.*

He rose early the next morning. Opening the back door, he was surprised to find Flannery curled up in one of the wicker chairs, a blanket that she had found somewhere wrapped around her. He approached and crouched down in front of her, his hand resting on her cheek.

"Hey, sleepyhead. Wake up."

Flannery's smile lit her face as she roused.

"Hi!" Her own hand rested on his. "You're up."

"I am. How long have you been out here?"

She shrugged. "I don't know. I couldn't sleep and walked the area around Eunice and Everett's. Then somehow, I made my way here. Around five or so? The sky was just starting to lighten."

"Flannery! You could have disappeared, you know!"

She shrugged, shoving him away so that he could rise.

"And good morning to you too!" She stepped away, ready to head back home when his hand stopped her.

"I'm sorry. I didn't mean to speak that harshly. But it's true."

"I know. Don't you think I know that?" She spun, tears on her cheeks. "It's just that today is the anniversary of when

Mom died. No matter what she was, she was still my mother. I miss having someone who really cared about me."

Evan gave an inaudible sound and then swept her into a hug.

"I'm sorry, sweetheart. What can I do for you?"

"Don't leave me. Please don't leave me."

Evan heard the plea in her voice, and it broke his heart. His anger grew at the man who was responsible for this before he had to acknowledge that while he could be angry, he needed to let God have it and work out bringing the man to justice.

"I won't, sweetheart. I won't." He wrapped her tighter in his arms. "What am I do to with you? You wander around at night, all by yourself."

"Not by myself. Sam was with me. I sent him home just before you came out." Flannery leaned back. "You're just getting up?"

"No, to tell you the truth, I never slept. I spent the night in prayer, sweetheart."

———

"You did? And did you get any answers? Any answers that we can work with?"

Evan shook his head even as he smiled. He caught movement to his left and looked up, a hand raised to Everett. Everett nodded and then pointed back the way he had come before he turned. That Everett and Eunice were worried was a given.

"Did you leave a note?"

Flannery looked at him, shocked. "No. I didn't. I should have. I'm sorry. I just walked away." She sighed, her head going down against his chest, hearing the strong steady beat of his heart. "I'm not used to someone watching out for me."

"There is this time, sweetheart. Here, let me grab my stuff and we'll head that way. Eunice said that Lydia may arrive today, tomorrow at the latest."

"She will? Oh, I guess then I'll need to move on."

"Not at all. Lydia called me, asking for a ride home from town when she gets in. She is eager to meet the lady who makes my voice sing."

"Your voice sings?" Flannery stared at him. "That's an odd thing to say."

"But it's the truth, sweetheart. The song in my heart caused by you has to come out." He turned her towards her home. "And we need to talk."

Flannery sighed. "That's all we seem to do, isn't it? Talk. Talk. Talk. And get nowhere."

"Actually, I had an email from my old sergeant. He's heading this way over the next couple of days with some information that he wants to go over with us both. He says it's important that we do this soon."

"About what?"

"About our adventure, sweetheart." Evan stopped her at the edge of the clearing, looking around before he swept her into another hug and kissed her. His mouth opened to apologize when her fingers stopped him.

"Don't apologize. If you do, then you didn't mean it."

"I did, sweetheart, but I should have asked."

"Ask away, but it's too late. You can't take it back." She swatted at his arm. "How dare you?" She ran, her smile stopping him for a moment before he laughed and then ran after her.

He caught her into his arms and claimed another kiss.

"Will you marry me?"

Flannery stared at him. "Two kisses and you want to marry? Evan!"

Chapter 24

Lydia stood for a moment, her mother's arm around her as she studied her home.

"It's good to be home, Mom. I like what you and Dad have done here."

"It's been work but we're set now. Your bedroom is done in your favourite colours with your own bed and dresser and whatnot from the old house. You said you wanted them."

"I do, Mom. I did. You and Dad have been okay?" Lydia knew that her mother was worried about something and she had a good idea what it was.

"We are, love. We are. Dad's out with Sam in the rowboat, trying to catch fish for supper. He's that determined to catch them. Evan will be here. But then you know that. He brought you home."

"He did. I wasn't sure on when I would get here. When we were talking the other night, I asked if he would give me a lift home. He agreed. He sounds different." Lydia frowned at the change she sensed in her friend.

"He has, Lydia. He's in love and his lady is in danger."

"Oh, dear! That would do it. He'll not back away until she's safe." Lydia looked around. "Where are they?"

Evan stood for a moment watching Lydia.

"I'm here, Lydia." He grinned as she made a face at him. "Flannery is at work." He glanced at the clock. "Early finishing today, Eunice?"

Eunice began to laugh. "Go and see if it works. I tried and she just refused."

Evan grinned. "I have a secret weapon." He walked away to Lydia's question of just what that would be.

Eunice hugged her daughter. "More than likely kisses. Now, we are in a situation that you may be able to help us with. Flannery ran from someone that we think was going to make her into a mule at the very least."

"A mule?" Lydia's face paled. "That's not good. That's what I work against. Evan is involved?"

"He is. He rescued her and brought her to us. They've had some trouble, but we fear it's just beginning."

"More than likely it is." Lydia stared at her mother before she looked towards the hallway. She said a name, catching the look on her mother's face. "I couldn't say anything, Mom. It's been too dangerous for the people I'm helping. That's why I was overseas. Working on that end. We've stopped the pipeline to him."

"And if he finds out you were involved, you are not safe." Everett hugged his daughter. "Look what I found for you!"

"Fish! Oh, Dad! You have no idea how I have longed for a home-cooked fish dinner. And yes, I am in danger. I am sure that he knows. And he will go after you two as well."

"I'm sure that he will." Everett headed back outside to clean the fish, Sam staying close to Lydia. That was until he saw Flannery and then he was off to rub against her.

———

Flannery stood, her hand in Evan's, uncertainty on her face as she watched Lydia. She was not good at meeting people, she thought. They were too ready to judge her.

Lydia turned at that moment, a question on her lips for Evan that died as she saw Flannery. She approached her and then just hugged her.

"Welcome to the family, Flannery. Did I say it right?"

"You did. It was a grandmother's maiden name. Mom chose it. Dad hated it. He called me "Hey, you"."

"That's not very nice." Lydia linked an arm with Flannery. "Come on. I want to see what they've done outside. Evan, you can come or stay." She grinned at him. "We're old friends, Flannery. I have a friend in the city. He's planning on heading this way next week for a couple of days."

"David is coming? Wonderful." Evan tailed the women, his eyes searching. He could feel someone out there.

"He is. Oh, I like those flowers."

"Flannery's handiwork." Evan was quick to give his lady the credit.

———

153

"You have a knack there, Flannery."
Lydia studied her. "I know you."

"You do?"

Lydia nodded. "I do. You were at a
church when I was. About two years ago. I
was speaking and you were just so intent on
listening. That made you stand out. You
were gone before I could get through the
crowd to you."

"I remember now. You spoke about
human trafficking and how drug dealers
will use the victims to advance the drug
trade."

"I did. I am so glad that Evan rescued
you. I know what happens, Flannery. Now,
Dad will be looking for us soon for dinner.
Any chance of canoeing, the three of us,
tonight?"

"We can. You in yours and Flannery
with me." Evan paused.

"But it's not a good idea, is it?" Lydia
sighed, turning Flannery back towards the
house. "I have to get used to this here. I'm
used to it in the city and where I was
overseas."

"I see. We need to talk then."
Flannery slipped away, sorrow in her heart

for what she knew Lydia had seen over the years.

Evan watched her before Everett spoke from beside him.

"Lydia said something?"

"She did. She has seen Flannery before. At a church where she spoke. I think that it upset Flannery when she realized that someone knew what her life had been like." Evan rubbed at his face.

"I see. Lydia won't let that come between them. They'll be good for each other." He started to walk away when Evan spoke. "What was that, Evan?"

"If Flannery lets her. She thinks that she's too dangerous to know." Evan sighed. "And I might as well tell you that I asked her to marry me. She asked for time to think about it, pray about it, and then talk to someone. I have no idea who that would be."

"Eunice likely. Maybe me? She seems to be thinking of me as a father figure."

"I'm glad, Everett. She needs that. With what she's going through."

"And just where does it stand?"

Evan drew in a deep breath. "I need to talk with you all. Tag and Dooley have been in touch. My old sergeant is on his way up in the next couple of days."

"Is that so?" Everett's eyes were on Flannery as she approached. "Just make sure you marry for the right reason, Evan. If you love her, tell her and often."

Chapter 25

Flannery was at a loss. Eunice had stopped working for a couple of days and she was all caught up. She sighed. Now what, Flannery? What do you do? She was on her feet, shoving them into her worn sneakers, and heading for the outdoors. The flowerbeds could always use some work, she thought.

She paused as she finally reached the one near the dock. It was disturbed, she could tell. Plants had been uprooted and then dumped back into place. She reached for one, digging into the dirt when her hand froze, and she tumbled backwards as she threw herself away. She retched and then was on her feet, running towards the house.

Everett had just stepped outside as he saw her. Her white face worried him, and he quickly shoved her into the house.

"Flannery? What is going on?" Everett stared between her and the door.

"A body!" She could barely speak.

"A body? What are you talking about?"

"In the flowerbed. Near the dock. A body." She stared down at her hands. "I touched him."

"Flannery, here. Wash up. Lock up after me. I'll be right back." Everett was out of the cabin, heading for the flowerbed. He stared down at the hand that showed in the dirt. *She's right. A body.* His phone was out as he called it in.

He turned an hour later as he heard Eunice and Lydia.

"Everett? What is going on? We couldn't drive in but they let us walk in with an escort."

"Flannery found a body in the flowerbed near the dock. She's in your office, curled up in a blanket."

Eunice looked at him and then Lydia.

"Come with me, Lydia. I'll need you to stay with her. I'm heading out to see what's going on."

Lydia watched Flannery carefully before she pulled out her phone.

"Evan? Where are you?"

"At home, Lydia. My sergeant got here this morning. Why?" Evan sounded distracted.

"Because your lady needs you. She found a body this morning, Dad says."

Evan froze, his eyes on his sergeant. "We'll be over. And we will come by the road,"

"Thank you, Evan. She's just sitting here, not speaking. And she's so white."

"Tell her I'm on my way. And don't let her go anywhere."

Flannery looked up at that point.

"You shouldn't have called him." Her voice was shaky and low.

"Yes, I should have. Dad should have and didn't." Lydia sat beside her, reaching to hug her.

"I wouldn't let him. I knew that Evan would be busy today. I didn't want to disturb him."

"This? Flannery, he would want to be here. For you. Don't you understand that? It's who he is. He would be here for a friend and even more so for you." Lydia stared at her for a moment. "He's in love with you, if you didn't know that."

"I know he is. He shouldn't be." Flannery's voice was barely a whisper, but loud enough that Evan heard her.

Evan was beside her, scooping her into his arms and sitting back in her spot.

"I will be here for you, Flannery. No matter what you're going through." His head went down on hers. "Having an adventure without me?"

Flannery gave him a disgruntled look.

"I am. I don't like it." She frowned as he grinned. "It's not funny."

"No, it's not. I understand that. It's just that you look so put out." His eyes raised as his sergeant from the old force approached. "Sweetheart, this is my old supervisor. He would really like to speak with you."

"About what?" Flannery was not feeling much like talking.

"About what happened to you. He thinks it's related to something that happened a few weeks ago to another lady."

She stared at the sergeant before she sighed. "I know you."

"You do. You helped out someone that I care about." He didn't say much more.

"Amie? She was uncertain about that teen. I talked to her, that's all." Flannery didn't want any credit or thanks.

"I know you did. Her mother and I want to thank you." His hand went up at her protest. "You saved her from who knows what. She finally opened up to us and talked to us. She was sad that you had disappeared."

"I'm glad that she's okay. Tell her that for me, please."

"I will be delighted to. She'll want to come and thank you herself."

Flannery shrugged, her eyes going towards Dooley. "It's okay. If I'm still here." She didn't see the look Evan gave her or the looks the others in the room shot towards them both. "Dooley? You're here."

"I am, Flannery. I had to just get in on your adventure." He gave a small smile.

"I don't want this adventure. Can you make it stop please?" Flannery knew that she was begging and asking for something that Dooley could not stop. Not at the present time at any rate.

"We would like to do just that, Flannery." Dooley hesitated for a moment before he had a seat. "We'll need to talk, Flannery. When you're up to it."

"And if I'm not?" Flannery buried her head against Evan, not wanting to look at anyone.

Chapter 26

Dooley simply nodded, a grim look on his face as he took a seat. Eunice had followed him with a tray of coffee for the men, tea for the ladies. She hesitated before Dooley looked at her and then at Flannery. She nodded, setting the tray to one side and sitting near Flannery.

"Dooley?" Flannery's voice was tight, her emotions under strict control. "What did you find?"

"The body. We don't have any identification on him yet. That will take time. It will take time for us to clear away from here." His notebook and pen were out. "Walk me through your day until that point."

Flannery sighed. "This is getting very old."

"I know it is. Okay, when you're ready." Dooley watched her, seeing how close to the edge she was. He shared a look with Evan, who simply nodded.

"Today? I was all caught up with what Eunice had for me. I decided to work in the gardens. That was the last one. Sam and I approached it and I saw the plants had been disturbed and just stuck back in however they got there. That wasn't how it was late last night. Evan and I walked that way after our supper and just spent time in the chairs near them. I went to replant the flowers and when I dug into the dirt, that's when I found the hand. Sam was upset and growling. I just ran for the cabin. Everett was waiting and rushed me inside. I don't know who it is. And I didn't do it."

"We know that, Flannery." Dooley's voice held conviction. "Whoever it is? This is a warning to you. Do you understand that?" He watched with compassion as her head nodded, her face pale.

"I do. I have seen too much, haven't I? Only I have no idea who or why. And is it really related to whoever it is you think it is?" Her eyes closed as she groaned. "That didn't make a whole lot of sense."

"It did. You're doing fine." Dooley tucked away his pad and pen. "We'll talk again, Flannery."

"That's what I'm afraid of. Maybe I should just leave town." She didn't look at anyone in the room and didn't see the look of devastation that briefly crossed Evan's face.

"That won't work, Flannery." Dooley was stern with her, knowing that she would run given a chance and that Evan would be right behind her. And that would leave him chasing after the pair of them to bring them back.

"It doesn't? I was hoping it would." Flannery grew quiet, settling back against Evan's shoulder, her eyes on the floor, not really listening to any of the conversations.

Joe, Evan's old supervisor, watched her closely. He had not realized how much danger his daughter had been in until she approached himself and her mother. He had looked for Flannery and not found her. He had even gone to the streets, asking around. The word he heard was that she had left town and that someone was after her. That had brought him to Evan's that day, needing to speak with him. Evan had told him what had transpired the day he left town. When he said the name Flannery, Joe knew that he had found the lady that he was searching for.

Dooley finally rose to leave, his mouth open to speak with Flannery before he snapped it closed. She knows what she is facing and is trying to save Evan from worrying about her. That will not work. He nodded to the gathering group and then walked out, Eunice following him.

"Dooley?" Her voice was quiet as they stopped just outside the back door, watching the activity that still filled the yard.

"I don't know, Eunice. I just don't know. I couldn't say anything to Flannery. But I know who it is. He's been on the edge of the law for years."

"He has?" Eunice murmured a name, Dooley just looking at her. "I see. Then, that's that, isn't it?"

"We need to watch Flannery, Eunice. I don't need to tell you that." Dooley's mouth drew into a grimace for a moment. "She'll run if given a chance."

"I know that she will. And we can't stop her." Eunice's hands rubbed at her upper arms. "Evan may be able to stop her but we can't even guarantee that."

"If she runs, he'll follow her. You do know that." Dooley's attention was on the activity near the dock. "I'm sorry, Eunice. This has invaded your home."

———

"It has but it can't be helped. We're not going to throw Flannery out of the house. You know us better than that."

Dooley gave a laugh. "No, you won't. But Evan may move in." He stopped, a thought crossing his mind. "How close are those two?"

Eunice shot him a puzzled look before her face cleared and she grinned. "Thinking that they'll marry so that he can protect her? He may try that. She's not ready."

"No, she's not. He is. I can tell just by how he looks at her and watches out for her." Dooley paused again. "I was surprised to see Evan's old supervisor."

"I was too." Eunice turned to watch the house. "He mentioned that Joe was coming up today. I never expected to meet him this way." She drew a deep breath. "How many teens has Flannery helped?"

"A lot, I would imagine. And that's likely why he's after her. His name on the street is The Duke."

"The Duke? Oh, he's been around for years. We've just never been able to nab him." Eunice's face grew worried. "And now someone who we know and love has become involved with him."

"I would say Flannery's been involved for years and that's why she's been moving so much. No one does that without a reason. She told me one day that she only stayed the most in a place for four or five months and then moved on. She didn't say why."

"Fear. Danger. We know that drill." Eunice finally moved back into the house, standing at the kitchen sink staring towards the lake. She sighed. *How do we do this, Lord? How do we solve this without one of them getting hurt? And that is such a danger. All we can do, dear Father, is to pray for Your protection on them.*

Chapter 27

Staring at the garden the next day, Flannery wrapped her arms around herself. She was terrified, she knew, and so afraid for Evan, Eunice, Everett, and now Lydia. She and Evan had not talked about her find. Flannery had simply walked away from him towards the end of the morning. Evan had watched her go, a sigh rising in him along with his fear. Joe had watched the two, concern in his heart for his young friends. And he considered Flannery part of his family, given that she had saved his daughter from so much danger.

Evan stood beside her, an arm wrapped around her to hold her close to himself. He didn't say anything. The fact of the matter was he didn't know what to say. Flannery leaned against him, drawing strength and comfort from him.

"Evan?" Her voice had a wobble to it.

"Flannery? What's up?" Evan tilted his head to watch her face, seeing the raw emotions on it. She rarely did that, he knew. Today was one of those days that she did.

"Why do I stay here? I'm such a danger to everyone." She turned her head up to watch him, finding him watching her closely. The look in his eyes caught her attention, saying that she was special and important to him. She frowned for a moment before her own face softened. Flannery was falling in love, without being aware of it.

"I won't let you leave me, Flannery. You are too important to me." Evan wrapped her into a hug. "I just can't." He bit at his upper lip for a moment. When he spoke again, his voice was barely audible but held his heart. "You would take my heart with you if you did."

Flannery's hands had been up against his chest to push herself away from him and stopped. *Did he really say that? Lord, I have no idea what this means but Eunice says that You love me and want the best for me. Does that mean a relationship with Evan?*

Evan stared past her, watching the lake, seeing its calmness that day. They were off to church shortly, but he had plans for that afternoon if the lake stayed calm.

He wanted very much to take Flannery to a favourite island in the centre of the lake, just a small one. A picnic lunch was ready in his fridge. His eyes turned to her upraised face, and he had just had to kiss her.

Flannery's eyes closed as he did so, not sure of anything anymore. She knew that she had to leave, and that very thought devastated her.

"I'm sorry, Flannery. I shouldn't have done that." Evan bit at his lip again. "At least not yet."

Flannery's puzzled gaze met his. "Not yet?"

"No, you're not ready for a relationship. And that's what I want. I want to explore where we could go as friends, to see if our friendship could deepen to something more."

"Something more? As in?" She had a suspicion on what he meant.

"As in dating, marriage." Evan gave a groan. "Did I really just say that?"

"You did. You're special, did you know that? And thank you." Flannery moved away, heading back for the cabin. "We need to leave soon."

Evan's head dropped for a moment before he ran after her.

"I know we do. And this afternoon, I would like to take you to a special place."

"A special place?" Flannery watched his face, seeing the softening of remembered events on it.

"There's an island in the lake. Dad and I used to go on impromptu picnics. I would like to take you there. Only it means going in a canoe."

"I see. And you plan on overturning that and dumping me into the lake to see if I can really swim?" She grinned at him. "I can. And yes, I will go."

That afternoon, Flannery stared at the canoe as Evan held it, ready for her to step in. I can do this, she scolded herself. I really can. I can swim too. Not well, but perhaps enough to keep myself afloat if this fragile thing tips over.

Evan watched her struggle with a grin on his face. He knew that she was hesitant but determined to do what he had asked.

"I promise, sweetheart. I won't tip you out of it. Not if I can help it. The lake is calm, really."

"Really?" She pointed at the waves. "That is calm? I think those things are called waves. And waves are dangerous." She smirked at his grin.

"Waves can be, but these are tiny, itty-bitty ones." He reached for her hand, helping her in and to a seat before he pushed the canoe from the shore and hopped in himself. "I won't ask you to paddle."

"You won't? Afraid I'll splash you?" Her hand was in the water, tossing some at him, a grin fixed on her face.

"Hey! That's not fair!" Evan gloried in her lightheartedness, knowing that she was trying her best to set aside the mystery surrounding her, watching her as she grinned and then looked towards the island.

"That's it?" She pointed with a slim forefinger.

"It is. It's not big. We can walk around it in less than thirty minutes."

"We can? Oh, I would like that. I enjoy walking. Except for lately. Then I always feel like someone is watching me or following me."

"They more than likely are." Evan was out of the canoe, pulling it up on the island shore, then reaching for her hand. "Out you come. Here, let me grab the pack with our lunch. This is nice, Flannery. Thank you."

Chapter 28

Reaching to pick up the backpack with their lunch, Evan slung it over a shoulder before he reached for Flannery's hand. The canoe had been pulled up high on the shore. He waited as she stood, staring at the area around her.

"This is nice. Who owns it?"

"I do. Dad bought it years ago for me."

"It's yours? How thoughtful of your father." She tugged at his hand. "Can we explore?"

"We can. Here. If we head this way, we can find the path that leads around the shore." Evan led her that way even as he was speaking, watching her face closely.

Her face raised to the sun, Flannery stopped for a moment, her eyes closing against the light. She sighed. *This is heaven, Lord. Somewhere I can relax without having to worry about anyone else.*

"Can I live here, Evan?" The plaintive tone in her voice caught at his heart.

"We could, but we would have very rudimentary facilities. You're not quite ready to give up yet."

She scowled at him before a finger pointed ahead of her.

"Aren't we supposed to be touring the island or something?" She frowned as she looked up once more, catching the few clouds that were moving across the sky. "Are we in for rain? I won't go in that fragile thing that you call a canoe if we are."

Evan grinned at her. "We're not supposed to. Not until tonight. Come on. Let me show you the cave Dad discovered."

Flannery stared at the shallow cave-like opening. It wasn't large, she decided, but it was cute. Just what a young boy would have liked. Her dreams had been to have a father like that. Only it hadn't worked out. She sighed to herself, feeling herself caught up in one of Evan's hugs.

"This is cool, Evan." Her voice was quiet when she finally spoke.

"Cool? I haven't heard that expression for a bit." His chin rested on the top of her head. "Dad looked for ways to make memories for me, to make up for Mom not being there. He always told me to follow my dreams."

"And you did. But your dreams chewed you up and spit you out." Flannery moved away from him. "What is your dream now, Evan?" She refused to look at him, afraid that she would see the look on his face that he didn't want anything to do with her anymore.

"I have a few, love. One is that you stay with me forever." Evan reached for her hand. "Come. Let's find the fire pit and we can eat. Then, we talk."

Later that afternoon, Evan reached to put out the fire. The clouds had thickened and darkened, and the wind had picked up. He sighed. Not the way that he wanted to head back across the lake, but they had to. A sudden streak of lightning lit up the sky, causing Flannery to jump and give a low cry.

"Evan? It's storming? We can't go back." Worry stood on her face.

"No, we can't. Come on. We'll head for the cave. Hopefully, we can stay

———

somewhat dry there. The rain is coming from the opposite direction." He grabbed for her hand and ran, just missing the rain as it started to fall. He tucked her into the cave and then stood watching before he reached into the backpack and drew out an emergency blanket.

"What is that?" Flannery couldn't think of what it was that he was holding.

"It's an emergency blanket. Here, we'll wrap you into it and tuck you behind me."

"No. I won't. Not if you don't have one."

Evan sighed and then moved her into the cave, wrapping the blanket around the two of them.

"Sit, Flannery. This will go under us. Hopefully, the storm will move through quickly." Evan didn't think it would, but he didn't want to panic Flannery any more than she was.

They watched the rain, words few and far between. Flannery's head finally went down against Evan and she slept. He sighed. This was not how their day was to end. He squinted at the rain. No, not at all.

———

It was late afternoon and into the evening before he roused Flannery, reaching to draw her to her feet.

"We need to leave now, love. There's a break in the storm and we can get to shore."

"It's too dangerous, Evan." Flannery resisted the pull on her hand. "Look at those waves."

"I know, love. But I'll head into the shore on a different route, one that's a lot shorter."

True to his word, Evan had them on the main shore in no time. He had smiled to himself at the tight grip that Flannery had kept on the canoe, her fingers white. He helped her ashore and then stashed the canoe up from the water.

"Your canoe? You can't leave it here!" Flannery was worried.

"I can, Flannery. It's on my property. So, it's safe. I'll retrieve it at a later time. Come on. We need to get you home."

"Home?" Flannery stared up at him for a moment. "Where's my home, Evan? I don't have one."

"You do, Flannery. You do. Right now, that's with Everett and Eunice. At some point, it is my dream that it's with me. But that has to be your dream as well."

Flannery stared at him for a moment. "Is that really your dream?" When Evan nodded, she simply reached to hug him. "Thank you, Evan. You make me feel special and wanted. I haven't had that in so many years, I can't remember when I felt that last."

Chapter 29

The next morning, Everett was on a hunt. He knew that Sam had alerted during the night to someone outside their cabin. He frowned for a moment as he looked around before he headed for the little workshop that he had. Pausing, Everett shook his head. Whoever it was had been around. He turned as Eunice approached.

"Everett? You're not going in? I thought that you had plans to work in there this morning." Eunice wrapped an arm around her husband's waist.

"I was. That was until I saw that." Everett pointed at the step to the workshop. "We'll need Dooley or whoever it is that's on duty today."

Eunice moved closer to study the box.

"It has no name on it but it is likely meant for Flannery. She'll just up and leave on us, I think."

Everett shook his head. "I don't think so. Evan told me that he has asked her to marry him but that she needed time to think and pray over it. That's a change for her, to ask for time to pray over something."

"He has? That would solve one problem but create another." Eunice stared towards the cabin. "She hasn't said much about yesterday other than she wanted to go and live on the island. Did Evan take her there?"

"I suspect so. Come on, love. We'll be in the way, or at least I will when help arrives." Everett led Eunice away even as her phone was out of her pocket to call in help.

An hour later, Dooley stared down into the box that he had opened before his head raised. He stared at the shed in front of him, not seeing it before he shook his head. He picked up the box and headed for his car, setting it on the trunk before he turned to Eunice.

"Eunice? Where did this come from?"

"We don't know and we don't know when. Overnight I would suspect as it wasn't there when we went to bed. Why?"

"It's not threatening. Not that I can see." He stepped aside so that Eunice could look into the box that they were discussing.

Surprise on her face, Eunice shook her head.

"I don't understand, Dooley. What is this?"

"That's what I would like to know. Where is Flannery?"

"Right behind you. What did you find that you need to talk to me about?" Flannery stood five feet behind him, her arms wrapped around herself. Evan was tight beside her, his arm around her.

Dooley studied her, sensing something different about her but not sure what.

"This box? Everett found it this morning. I'm puzzled, though, Flannery. It's not a threat. Not that I can see." He beckoned her forward. "Take a look."

Flannery moved slowly towards him, Evan keeping step with her before she paused. She prayed hard, asking for protection. Whatever was in that box scared her. That much she knew.

She finally peeked into the box, a hand covering her mouth as she stifled a scream.

"What is that? I have never seen it before." She stepped backwards, forcing Evan to move back with her.

"You haven't?" Dooley reached into the box and pulled out the blanket. It was a blanket for a crib, he decided, unfolding it and finding a letter addressed to Flannery folded inside it. He carefully reached for it, turning it over and over, finding nothing that would alarm him.

Flannery had been watching carefully, not sure what was up. Evan's prayer was breathed in her ear, and she sank back against him.

"Flannery? You are sure that you have never seen this before?" Dooley watched her closely, knowing that Eunice was doing the same. He could see Everett and Lydia nearby, watching their young friend as well.

"Never. I have no idea who that is. And I didn't plant it to scare myself."

"We know that, Flannery." Dooley was frustrated. He handed her the letter. "You need to open this."

Flannery shook her head. "No, you do it, please, Evan?"

Evan nodded, reaching for the pair of latex gloves Eunice was handing him. Snapping them on, he then took the envelope from Dooley, his eyes on Flannery.

"You have no idea what this is about?" His voice was quiet, confidence in her response evident in it.

"I don't. Make it go away, please, Evan."

He searched her face before his attention went to the envelope. Evan turned it over and over before he reached for the flap that had been tucked down into the envelope. He pulled out the folded paper, not sure what he would find.

Flannery shook, her fear that great. She had no idea what to expect. All she knew was that she was terrified of that letter. She heard Everett's prayer as he waited for her to move, knowing that she needed the protection that only God could bring her.

Chapter 30

Evan slowly unfolded the letter, his eyes on Flannery instead of the paper. He sighed to himself. *She's terrified, Lord, and I have no idea why. I mean, I know that there is someone after her.* He frowned, a thought niggling at his mind. *What if it wasn't the Duke after her? What if someone just wanted her to think that?* He shook his head mentally. That was something that he needed to talk to Dooley and Tag about, he was sure of that.

Flannery poked at the paper, bringing his attention to her.

"Are you going to read that or not?" She frowned at him as he shook his head.

"I intend to. Dooley? How sure are we that it is the Duke?" Evan shared a look with Eunice even as Dooley stared at him.

"The Duke? I thought that's who it was. Are you saying that you don't think so?" Dooley's voice was incredulous at the thought.

"I am." Evan sighed. "He's still in Toronto, from what Tag has discovered. Tag can't find any evidence that any of his people have been this way. So if it's not him, then who?"

"Then who?" Dooley sighed. "You just threw a monkey wrench into the works, you do know that, don't you?"

Evan gave a quick grin, feeling Flannery leaning against him, her face down on his arm.

"I did, didn't I?" He glanced at the letter and frowned. "Flannery? Who would know you best?"

She shrugged. "No one. Not unless you count yourself." She frowned at him. "Did you leave that for me?"

Evan shook his head even as a grin crossed his face.

"Nope. Not me. You do need to read this. This is something different from what you've been experiencing."

"Something different?" Flannery stared up at him, shock on her face. "You mean I have two people after me? What did I do to warrant that?"

"I have no idea. But that is certainly what this letter is suggesting." Evan watched her closely. "Let me read it to you and then we'll talk. I promise Dooley and Eunice can be involved. I think we need them to be."

Flannery shrugged. "Whatever. Can we sit? I don't think my knees will last."

"We can." Evan's hand helped her to a chair, and he watched as the others sat around them. "Ready?"

"No!" Her voice was disgruntled. "But you're going to read it anyway, aren't you?"

"I am. We need to." He looked around. "Everett, can you pray? I think we need that."

Evan finally unfolded the letter again. "It's handwritten, Flannery. I would gather by someone older, just by the style of the writing." He prayed as he watched her, seeing her face shutter as he spoke. "Okay, then. Here we go."

His eyes dropped to the letter and he had a sudden vision of danger coming at her from more than one person. His heart fell as he thought through that. That's what he had felt all along.

<hr>

"Evan?" Flannery's quiet voice raised his head, and he shook it at her, mentally clearing away whatever it was that he had felt.

He looked down at it, a prayer rising in his heart, a prayer for his lady's protection. He could feel the walls of danger closing in on them.

"Flannery

"You do not know me, but I have followed you for years, watching as you have grown from a young child to an adult. This blanket is one that I used to tuck you into bed at night when I watched you. You see, I am your great-aunt. I have tried for years to reach out to you but have not succeeded. I have been prevented from that.

"The woman who has done that? She is evil and destructive. She has been behind your moves around the province. She has prevented me from coming to your province. How? That is a matter now of police investigation.

"Just know that this blanket has been held onto with love for you.

"Your great-aunt Martha."

Flannery stared at Evan as he finished, a puzzled look on her face.

"I don't have a great-aunt. Dad and Mom were only children. Their parents were only children. So who is she?"

Evan nodded, his eyes on Dooley and then Eunice.

"You two have researched her family?" At their nod, he sighed. "Flannery is correct? Then who is this person?"

Flannery shoved away from Evan, panic in her voice.

"Get rid of that, please, Evan? It's dangerous. I just know it is." Flannery was on her feet, running for the house, the door swinging closed behind, Sam tight to her as she flung herself onto her bed.

Chapter 31

Evan approached Flannery the next day, not quite sure of what was going on with her. She had been withdrawn after she had reappeared the previous day, not joking with him as she had been.

"Flannery?"

"Go away, Evan. I can't be around you." Flannery stood staring at the lake, her arms wrapped around herself.

"Not happening, Flannery. Now, we need to talk."

She spun, her words biting at him. "That's all we do. Talk. Where is the man or woman who is after me? How do we find them?" She spun around from him and walked away, leaving him staring at her before he ran towards her, a hand on her arm to stop her.

"Don't run from us, Flannery."

"I have to, Evan. You are in danger because of me." She bit at her lip. "No one can tell me who it is that I am supposed to be afraid of and avoid. Why not?"

"Because we don't know for sure. That's part of what Dooley and Eunice are working on. It takes time."

"Time that we may not have." Flannery's eyes searched the woods. "Evan, there's someone out here."

"I know. We need to get you to safety." Evan's words died away as he saw the shock on Flannery's face and then felt the dig of something into his back. *Please, Lord?* His heart cried out for protection for his lady even as he was shoved forward.

Flannery had stared at the man behind Evan before she was spun and had propelled forward, barely keeping her balance. She heard Evan's protest at her rough handling, a protest that died quickly away. She walked forward, tripping over branches and rocks, a rough hand on her arm keeping her upright.

Evan watched closely, hoping to find a way to escape but he knew that would be unlikely to happen. His heart sank as he saw the direction they were taking. It was away from town and towards an old homestead that had sat for years, in ruins. The town had tried to condemn it but the taxes were paid. The absentee landowner had seen to that.

The young couple were shoved once more forward, barely able to keep to their feet from the force of the push. Evan's hand reached for Flannery's, finding hers cold and clammy as she gripped his in turn. The room that they were shoved into was dark. Both could feel the dampness and heard the groans of the ramshackle building as it protested the presence of outsiders. The door was slammed behind them and both heard the sound of a heavy bar sliding down into place.

Evan hesitated for only seconds before he was searching the room, trying his best to find a way out. He pried at the boards covering the windows, the broken glass in them taunting them. He finally stood, a hand to his cheek, his eyes on Flannery.

Flannery was angry, angrier than she thought she had ever been. She was angry that someone had come onto the property that she considered home and put her friends at risk. She was angry that Evan was with her and that his life likely was in danger. Then she sighed to herself. Anger didn't work, she knew. It wouldn't get her

---

out of there. *Lord, You are here. You have promised to never leave me or forsake me. Please protect my Evan. Take him back to where he belongs, with his friends. I don't think that I will live to make it out of here.*

Evan simply wrapped Flannery into his arms, a prayer whispering in her ears that calmed her. Her arms around him, she struggled to control her emotions before she finally spoke.

"Did you find a way out?"

"Not yet, but I will." Evan stared at the door. "We can't get out that way."

"This would be a good time for one of your father's hidden tunnels or hiding spots."

Evan gave a brief laugh even as a grim look crossed his face. "It would be, sweetheart. It would be. Let me see what I can do."

Evan moved towards the door finally, his hands searching it, trying to find a way through it without success. He could hear Flannery muttering to herself as she too searched for an egress from the room. Spinning as he heard an exclamation from her, he was across the room, his hand on her back.

"What did you find?" He frowned as she turned.

A look of surprise coloured her face. "This? It's a door. At least, I think it is a door. It was hidden in this closet." Flannery looked up at him. "Is it a way to escape?"

Evan set her gently aside and then stopped, his head bowed as he whispered a barely audible prayer. He pulled at the swollen wood and then stopped, looking around.

"What do you need?" Flannery held out an old knife, whose blade had rusted. "Is it something like this?"

"It is, sweetheart." Evan reached for it even as he kissed her. "Pray that it works, sweetheart. Listen for someone coming."

"There won't be. They'll leave us here to die. No one would find us." Flannery chewed at her lip. "I just don't get it."

"I don't either." Evan worked away at the door, chipping off the rotten wood until he had enough removed that the door slid towards him, a rusty creak sounding loudly in the air. "Let's pray that they didn't hear anything."

Flannery's hand was on his back. "I haven't heard anyone moving around. I think they just dumped us here. And just where is here, anyway?"

"It's an abandoned property not far from my place. They really didn't walk us that far. It just seems that way. If we can get out, I know a way home that isn't the way we came."

"You do? Of course, you do." Flannery's hand pushed at him. "Well? What are you waiting for?"

"It's almost night, Flannery. That could work to our advantage. Just let me check out things." Evan hesitated at the edge of the house, his feet careful in how he placed them in the dried leaves and debris under them. "Okay. It looks good." He turned to find Flannery holding onto the knife that he had handed her as he worked the door open. "Armed, are we?"

"I am. And I shut the door behind us. Let's pray that they don't come back anytime soon."

Chapter 32

Everett had been on a hunt for the younger couple. He stood in the centre of the dock, a frown on his face, even as Sam paced around him, a low growl coming from his companion.

"They are not here, Sammy. Where are they?" Everett moved back towards the house, stopped in his tracks as he saw a phone on the ground. He reached for it. He turned it over in his hand, realizing it was Flannery's.

Eunice walked towards him. "Everett? What is going on?"

"This." He held up the phone. "It's Flannery's. There is no sign of either her or Evan. And Sam's upset again."

"They're gone? Have you checked Evan's?" Eunice spun in a circle. "No, he would have told us if he was heading back that way. He always does." She sighed as she reached for her phone. "It's getting late,

Everett. Lydia has our supper ready but somehow, I don't think we'll be eating."

"Mom? Dad? Where's Evan? And Flannery?" Lydia stood beside them, a questioning look on her face.

"They're gone, love. And we just found that out. When did you last see them?"

Lydia shrugged. "Around noon, I think. I went into town not long after that. They've disappeared, haven't they?" She sighed. "When does it end for them?"

Dooley listened closely as Everett gave his statement.

"They're not at Evan's?"

Everett shook his head. "No. I was that way while we were waiting for you." He looked up at the sky. "If they're outside, they'll be in the rain that's moving in."

"I know." Dooley gave a frustrated sigh. "What is it with those two?"

"Evan will not abandon Flannery. His heart is involved. Hers is too." Eunice wrapped her arms around herself. "She just won't admit it yet."

"She has, Mom. She's just too afraid of Evan being hurt because of her." Lydia's arm was around her mother. "Can we move inside?"

Dooley nodded, watching at the three moved away from him before he turned to a fellow officer.

"Daniel?"

"We've tracked them towards the old Woods' place. I've been in touch with the judge and he's authorizing us to go in if we have to."

"Good. Then, let's head that way." Dooley squinted at the sky. "I hope we get there before the rain hits."

"I doubt that we will." Daniel shouldered his pack and moved away, his steps rapid as he did so.

Dooley paused for a moment, his eyes on the cabin, a hand raised to Eunice. He knew that she would stay there, waiting for word from them.

Daniel paused at the end of the overgrown clearing and stared at the ramshackle house.

"It's really fallen in since I was out a couple of months ago." Dooley nodded in agreement as Daniel moved forward.

"I'm not even sure that it's safe to go inside." Dooley moved around the building. "Daniel? Here! Those are footprints."

"They are. A man and woman, by the looks of it." He spun to stare at the building and pointed. "A door. Is that where they came out of?"

"It looks like it." Dooley moved towards it, watchful as he did so. The door creaked open as he shoved at it. "They were in here." He looked up as he heard a noise, and his weapon was on. "Police. Come out now."

The two abductors shared a look, shook their heads and moved forward. They were searched, their weapons removed from them, and then handcuffed. Daniel moved away to call for reinforcements. He sighed as he turned. Being such a small force, someone would have to come in from off duty to help but he knew that there would be no hesitation.

Eunice approached Dooley, her eyes on the two men, a frown in place before it cleared. She knew the men. They had been hanging around town for the last week or so.

"What do we have, Dooley?"

"These two, for starters. They don't belong here. We have them for trespassing at the very least. Daniel's been in through the building. We can see other tracks, male and female, in a locked room. They appear to have found this door and chipped away at it until they could get it open." Dooley spun in a circle. "I don't know where they went to, though."

"If it's Evan, he knows a lot of obscure trails in the area. He was adventurous as a youngster, always exploring. His dad had a time with him for a while." Eunice nodded at the men. "They've been hanging around town. Do you have any identification on them?"

"I do."

When Dooley spoke the names, Eunice shot a look at them and then gave a grim nod.

"They don't work for the Duke, but they do for a competitor. And that competitor is one we have been looking at. Word just came in that he is back in the area."

"He is? Of course, he is. But how does that relate to Evan or even Flannery?"

"That I don't know. Joe, Evan's old supervisor, is working on that as is Tag. I'm not sure now how much this is related to Flannery, or if somehow they've been connected through something."

"That could well be, Eunice, given that Evan was on the streets and undercover. He may have seen or heard something in passing that he doesn't remember."

"That's what I am afraid of." Eunice looked around. "Are you heading for the trail?"

"I am. Daniel and I will. If you would stay here while the scene is processed." Dooley turned as he heard footsteps. "And here is George, ready to take our prisoners in for us."

Chapter 33

Eunice watched as Dooley and Daniel moved off towards a narrow, overgrown pathway, seeing them pause for a moment of conversation before Dooley took the lead. She squinted up at the sky, her eyes closing briefly against the drizzle that was falling. She tugged her cap down tighter on her head and then headed for the house. Eunice knew that she would be the one to collect the evidence and it would take time to sort it out from the debris littering the place.

Dooley paused for a moment, frustrated as he felt the dampness dropping down and the darkness closing in. He didn't want to leave, not if he was close to the couple and that he felt he was. His heart raised in prayer for Evan and Flannery, knowing that given the circumstances, it would be God who led Daniel and himself to the couple. He prayed it would be soon. He had no idea where they were, if they were hurt, or even if they had managed to make their way home.

Daniel's hand on his shoulder stopped Dooley in his tracks and he turned, watching as his companion pointed off the trail.

"The trail breaks off here, Dooley. Did they go that way?"

Dooley swiped at the moisture on his face. "They may have." He searched ahead of where he had stopped and returned. "I don't see any disturbance ahead of us. Let's take it for now. Lead on, Daniel."

Daniel nodded, taking a swig from his water bottle, and then reaching for his large flashlight. "We're going to need these. Pray that we find them and soon, Dooley. If we don't and have to wait for daylight, I'm afraid of the condition that we'll find them in."

Daniel came to an abrupt halt, his hand up. His head turned as he heard soft muttering, pain in it, he thought. Now, where was it coming from?

Dooley moved to stand beside him, his own head turning as he listened.

"That sounds like Flannery. But where?" He suddenly pointed and was off, moving as quickly as he could, Daniel on his heels.

"Here, Daniel." Dooley was on his knees beside Evan's body, fear in his heart. His eyes raised to study Flannery, who was cuddled as tight to Evan as she could get, trying to keep him warm and dry, her arm around him. He saw the tears on her face, tears that mingled with the rain on it. "Flannery?"

Flannery didn't respond to his question and Dooley stared up as Daniel dropped down beside her.

"Flannery? Daniel's going to move you back from Evan. Just relax and let him."

His hands searching for any injury on Evan, he paused as he felt the side of Evan's head.

"Dooley?" Daniel's hands had hesitated at Flannery's ankle. "I think she has a fracture here." He shot a look at Evan. "How is he?"

"He's got a head wound. How bad, I can't tell yet." Dooley sat back. "We have no option. We can't leave them out here all night." He studied Flannery for a moment before his eyes dropped back on Evan. His hands were reaching for the first aid kit in his backpack, the roll of white bandage out so that he could wrap it around Evan's head, to try and stop the slow trickle of blood that trailed down the side of his head.

"No, we can't. I think we're close to the road now." Daniel's phone was out and he was calling for Eunice. "Eunice? We've found them. We're near Settler's Road. They're both injured."

"I'm on my way. I'll have an ambulance meet us at the main road. They'd never make it down that road, not in the rain. How bad?"

"Flannery has an injured ankle. Evan is unconscious. Dooley says a head wound." Daniel watched Dooley as he continued to assess the young couple, a tensor bandage out to wrap around Flannery's injured ankle.

Eunice grimaced as she slid behind the wheel of her vehicle. "Okay. On my way. How long for you to reach the road?"

"Not long. We just don't like moving them." Daniel was frustrated, having found the pair alive but injured.

"I don't think we have a choice, Daniel." Eunice clicked off her phone and then reached to call for an ambulance. Please, Lord, protect these two. Heal them. Let there not be too much in injury for them.

Daniel carefully lifted Flannery away from Evan, then helped Dooley pull Evan to his feet and then over Dooley's shoulder. A deep groan came from the injured man and the two officers exchanged worried looks. Daniel turned to sweep Flannery up into his arms, his flashlight in his hand to light their way. A short walk later and they were on the road, finding Eunice just pulling up. She was out of her vehicle to help.

"Dooley? Evan?" She was concerned about her young friend, to say the least.

"He's hurting, Eunice. We need to get them seen to."

"I know. Everett is here. He'll assess them and then we'll head out."

"That's great. Everett, where do you want them?" Dooley turned to the older man, finding Everett reaching to help with Evan.

Everett peered at him through the darkness and the heavier drizzle.

"Evan in my car. You'll be driving, Dooley. Daniel, you and Flannery with Eunice. The ambulance will meet us at the highway entrance." Everett's heart raised in prayer for his young friends, not sure how badly they were injured. He moved to assess Flannery, his hands gentle on the ankle, finding her wincing and trying to draw back from his touch. He shook his head, wrapping the ankle back into the bandage.

"Everett?" Daniel's voice was quiet. "Is that her only injury?"

"I don't know, Daniel. We won't know until we get them into the hospital. Pray that it is." Everett quietly shut the car door, watching as Eunice drove off before he headed back for his own vehicle, sliding onto the back seat beside Evan, his eyes on his young friend. "Off we go, Dooley."

"It will be a rough drive, Everett." Dooley shot a look back at Evan. "And that will be hard on him."

"We don't have any choice, Dooley. Head off. Eunice has the ambulance waiting for us. That's good."

A short while later, Everett helped to transfer Evan onto the waiting stretcher, his eyes finding Flannery already into the

ambulance. He climbed up himself, an arm
around Flannery to help stabilize her for the
trip to the nearby medical facility.

Chapter 34

Everett paced the small waiting room of the local hospital, his thoughts on his two friends. Daniel and Dooley had left after promising to return. He knew Lydia was around, likely in the chapel. His head raising as he heard footsteps, he reached to hug Lydia before taking the cup of coffee she had found for him.

"Any word yet, Dad?" She pulled him to a seat near the doors.

"Not yet. Your mom is with Flannery. She was out briefly but didn't say much."

Lydia's head rested against her father. Evan, she worried about. *He was an old friend, more of a brother*, she thought. *Flannery?* Now that was a lady hard to get to know but given how she had lived, Lydia could understand that. They had begun to talk, those two young ladies, Flannery gradually opening up.

They both looked up as they heard footsteps and then Eunice dropped down into a seat beside Everett, whose arm swept her close to him.

"What's the word, love?"

Eunice took a moment to pray for her friends and gather her thoughts.

"Evan has a head wound. Concussion more than likely, Phil thought. They'll monitor him for a while and then release him to us. We're listed as next of kin apparently."

"And Flannery?"

"Flannery? She has no next of kin, so I asked Phil to put us down after Evan. He looked at me when I asked that. Given the way Flannery and Evan are moving towards one another, I thought it only right. She has no one else." Eunice sipped at the cup of tea she held. "She has a fractured ankle, as Daniel thought. Exposure, but no hypothermia. God was looking after them."

"And she'll come back with us. Have either of them roused?"

Eunice shook her head. "Neither one. And we need them to. Only I'm not sure how much they will remember."

"That's too true, love." Everett's eyes closed for a moment as he drew a deep breath. "You collected all the evidence you could?"

"We did, as much as we could. Every officer came in to help as soon as they heard it was Evan. I don't think he understands how well thought of he is in the community."

"No, I don't think he does. He's there for everyone who needs his help or support without him thinking of himself." Everett looked up as Phil approached. "Phil?"

"Everett. Lydia. Eunice, we've set Flannery's ankle, but she has roused and is beginning to panic. If you or Lydia could come in?"

"We can, but we need Everett. She listens to him as she would to her father if her father had been like Everett."

The trio rose and followed Phil, hesitating for a moment in the doorway before Everett approached Flannery, laying a hand on hers and praying aloud for her.

Flannery roused somewhat, her eyes flickering open before pain drove her back into the darkness. She thought she heard herself prayed for but wondered at that. She didn't know anyone who would pray for her. Not anymore and then she wasn't sure if she really had had.

Evan's head turned restlessly on the pillow as Eunice approached him. Her hand rested on his forehead, stilling his motions. His eyes flickered and then stayed open as he squinted around.

"Evan? You're awake?"

"I think I am. Eunice? Where am I?"

"You're in our local hospital, Evan. Do you remember what happened?"

Evan stared at her through pain-filled eyes. "Not particularly. What day is it?"

"It's Sunday morning. You and Flannery went missing yesterday."

"Flannery? Who's that? I don't think that I know a Flannery." He dropped off into a natural sleep, Phil standing at the other side of the stretcher and watching.

"He doesn't remember? How close were they?" Phil looked up as Eunice hesitated.

"They're in love with one another. He's sure. She's not. I know that he did ask her to marry him, but she hadn't answered yet." Eunice sighed. "And I just know that

———

she's going to try and take off, even with the fractured ankle." She turned to walk away, leaving Phil staring after her before he shook his head.

Everett turned his head as Eunice approached him, his hands resting on the side rail to Flannery's bed.

"Evan?"

"He was awake but not really alert." Eunice sighed. "He doesn't remember Flannery at the moment."

Everett stared at her before a sound from Flannery drew his attention back to her.

"She's been rousing, love, but she's not quite awake."

Eunice nodded. "And we have to deal with what she just went through. Dooley will be around in the morning, he said. I have to work, but you'll be here?"

"That's a given. She's become like our own daughter, Eunice. We have to take care of her." Everett's arm drew his wife closer to him. "We need to wrap them in prayer, Eunice. This is far from over."

"I know. We have been, but I know it's just going to get much worse. God is there, as He has promised, but sometimes it's hard to see." Eunice's head rested against her husband. "How do we do this?"

"God will lead us and protect them. It may not seem as if He is, but He does. We've seen it so many times over the years."

"That we have, given our lines of work. He has been there." Eunice looked back at the door. "And He protected Lydia. Somehow, though, I fear for her, that she will become wrapped up in this adventure these two are on."

Chapter 35

Not looking at Eunice who stood in front of her, Flannery watched Evan as he dropped down onto the couch across from her. She was frustrated, to say the least, that this had happened. She was also terrified. The man who had assaulted Evan and threatened to kill him in front of her had been very forceful in his words. Flannery shrank against the chair back, knowing that she had to leave there and her friends, but knowing that she just couldn't do that at present. Not with a cast on her foot. She sighed to herself, questioning where God was in all of this.

Eunice's eyes studied her young friend, seeing the pain on her face but also something in her eyes. She's scared, Eunice thought. And she's not saying what happened.

"Flannery? What happened out there? You do need to talk to us, to give us your statement." Eunice sat beside her, notebook out.

Flannery kept her eyes on Evan before she shook her head.

"I don't remember all of what happened, Eunice. I remember us walking away from that building but then I don't know what happened."

Evan studied her, knowing that she was not telling all that happened.

"Who threatened you, Flannery?" Her eyes shot back up to his from where she had been looking at the floor. "And who did he threaten?"

A shuttered look came over Flannery's face and she dropped her eyes, knowing that Evan would read them only too well. He had gotten to know her that well. *Lord, I can't do this, she thought. I have to leave here, to keep them all safe. Only, I don't know how I ever will.* She was on her feet, her crutches thumping across the floor as she moved towards her bedroom, ignoring Evan's soft call after her.

Evan stood for a moment, his eyes on her before he dropped back to the couch, his head in his hands. He had a pounding headache and that he didn't really need at the moment. He was so afraid for the love of his life but just why, he couldn't say.

Lord, protect her. I fear for her very life, but I know that You have her in Your hands. Help me to trust You in this. It's so hard.

Eunice moved to follow Flannery, her eyes assessing her. Everett stood where he could watch her as well, shaking his head, knowing that she was planning on running and just how she planned to do that, he wasn't sure.

Sighing deeply, Evan pulled a blanket over himself, his head on the pillow Lydia had given him. His eyes shut, the light hurting them, even though it was now early evening and the lights in the cabin were dim. He dropped off to sleep, a troubled sleep in which Flannery and he were running. His body twitched with his dreams, Everett studying him closely.

Early the next morning, Flannery was on the dock, her eyes on the lake and the waves the wind was driving towards the shore. She shivered but not from the coolness of the wind. She was deeply afraid. Turning slightly to watch the cabin, she sighed to herself, something that she seemed to be doing a lot lately. *Lord, I guess we're on speaking terms. I just don't want Evan or the family here hurt and I just know that is what will happen. Protect*

———

218

them, dear Lord. Help me to find this man or woman or whoever it is that has been chasing me for years, it seems. I just want this over, please, Lord? I couldn't handle Evan or Eunice or Everett or Lydia being hurt because of me. I just know that I have to leave.

Lydia appearing beside her startled Flannery, causing her to jump. She stared at her, her eyes huge. Lydia simply grinned and handed her the mug she had been holding for her.

"I love this time of the morning. It's fresh, clean, and calm."

Flannery snorted, causing Lydia to grin.

"I don't think that lake is calm. Those are waves. And waves are dangerous."

Lydia laughed. "Those are truly waves. Not as big as I have seen here." Lydia sipped at her tea before she spoke. "Don't run, Flannery. Please? None of us want you to end up on the streets again and on your own."

"I have to, Lydia. I've brought danger to you all."

Lydia sipped at her coffee once more.

———

"Perhaps. But perhaps we've brought it to you. Evan will never tell you what he has seen on the streets. You do know that he was undercover for a number of years?'

Flannery nodded. "He did say that. In fact, I think I saw him at one point in his town when I was there. This is hard, you know."

"I know it is. I have seen it here in this country and overseas." Lydia's hand drew Flannery back to the chairs. She sat, her eyes on the troubled lake, her own thoughts just as troubled. "I can't talk to Mom and Dad. I know they are worried, but I can't worry them more. I think the man who is after you? He's the one I've been fighting against. We're in this together, Flannery, without either one of us realizing that."

"We are?" Flannery grew silent, her thoughts troubled as she thought back through what all she had faced. "Has God protected us, Lydia?"

"I have no doubt that He has and that He will. We may not like what we have to go through, but He is there. Every second." Lydia's head turned to watch Flannery, seeing how she was struggling to understand. "I know that is a difficult concept to grasp. I have trouble with it at times."

"I know. I just wish my life had been different. I had dreams when I was tiny, dreams of where I wanted to go, what I wanted to do or be when I grew up. Those dreams are gone." Flannery's voice died away as she made her confession. "So, Lydia, how do we find this man?"

Lydia shared a look with her. "You want to try and find him?" At Flannery's nod, Lydia set her mug down and then sat forward. "Okay. We'll pool our resources and see what we can do." She shot a look behind her. "We just need to keep Mom and Dad out of it. Evan? He'll want to be involved."

"I can't let him, Lydia. He'll be dead." Flannery's face crumpled for a moment as she fought tears.

"Is that what you were told?" At Flannery's nod, Lydia was up out of her chair and hugging Flannery. "That's what they all say. And you won't say anything to anyone. I know you won't."

Chapter 36

Hearing a slight noise near her, Flannery spun, her cast hitting her crutches and knocking them to the ground. Her hands covered her mouth, stopping the cry for help. Lydia was on her feet, not sure what exactly was happening before she too turned and then paled. She knew the three men who were standing in front of them and she didn't think that they were there for the good of the ladies' health.

"You're coming with us. Both of you. The boss wants to have a talk with you." The older of the men pointed towards the road. "Right that way, ladies."

Lydia hesitated and then moved to help Flannery, drawing back as a sharp blow fell on her arm. Flannery shook her head at Lydia, reaching for her crutches and then thumping away towards the road. Fear rose in her heart, fear for Lydia and then for the three still in the cabin. She knew there would be no sign left of their leaving, other than their mugs sitting on the arms of the deck chairs.

Flannery shifted slightly to stare back through the car window, watching as the cabin disappeared from sight in the early morning light. She felt Lydia's hand on hers, gripping it tightly. Neither of the young women knew where they were heading, only knowing that they were on their own. As handicapped as she was, Flannery knew that she could not run. Her mind spun with being captive again. This time, she just knew that they would not escape so easily. For one thing, she could not run. Not being on crutches.

Lydia had reached for Flannery's hand, finding it cold. She studied the men in the front of the car and then the man sitting beside Flannery. She frowned. They were known to her. Lydia just wasn't sure why she had been taken, except that she was with Flannery at the time.

Flannery's eyes roamed the area outside of the truck. It didn't appear that they were going too far from Everett's or even Evan's, but she could not be sure. She prayed as she had never prayed in her life, petitioning God to let Lydia go. She really wasn't sure why Lydia had been taken, other than she had been with Flannery.

Lydia drew in a deep breath as she saw the car turn onto a private road and then pause as one of the men jumped down and ran to open the gate, swinging it closed behind them and then regaining his seat in the front. There had been no conversation between the men.

The two young ladies were pulled from their seats and shoved towards a building at the back of the yard. Flannery struggled with her crutches on the lawn, finding it hard to balance herself. Lydia was prevented from helping her, her arm caught in a tight cruel grasp. They were shoved into the building, the door slammed behind them and then locked.

Flannery and Lydia stared at one another, horror and shock on their faces for a moment before Lydia spun, heading for the windows, trying her best to open them. They both knew they couldn't get out of the door. That was a given.

Flannery balanced on her crutches, her right foot in the cast held up in the air. She was tired and sore and in pain and had nothing that she could take for it. She stared around the large room.

"This is strange, Lydia. It's like a guest suite."

"I know." Lydia has searched the whole building, finding two bedrooms and a bathroom off the great room as she decided it was called. A small kitchen sat at the end of the room.

"I don't like this, Lydia. Who are they?"

"The men? I know who they are." Lydia's finger was on her mouth, signaling Flannery to be careful in how she spoke. "The fridge is stocked with food. It's like they knew we would be here."

"I think they did." Flannery maneuvered over to drop down on the couch, her foot upon it. She rubbed at her leg. "They were waiting for us, I think, Lydia. They wanted both of us. But why?"

Flannery frowned, her eyes on the door located on the front wall of the house, the one that they had been shoved through before she moved towards it. Her hand rested on it for a moment before she tried the knob. The knob turned under her hand, but the door just didn't open. She turned back to Lydia, who stood, her eyes on Flannery.

"Flannery? What are you planning?"

Flannery shrugged. "I have no idea what I am planning. We need to find a way out." Her crutches thumped across the floor as she made her way to the back door and opened it, balancing on her crutches. "A yard but what a high fence!"

Lydia peered around her. "It is. At least we can get outside. But that has to be what seven or eight feet high." She moved outside and spun in a circle. "There is no way we can climb over it, I don't think, Flannery. Not with you in a cast."

"I know. I was hoping there would be a way." Flannery slumped down into one of the chairs on the patio. "I want out of here, Lydia. How do we do this?"

Lydia shook her head. "I don't know. And I can almost guarantee that they are listening in on our conversation."

Chapter 37

Evan finally stirred, a hand coming to rub at his eyes, as he listened to the quiet conversation between his two friends. He raised up to sit on the couch, a hand rubbing at his face in turn as he listened to the morning sounds filtering through the windows. He sighed. He hurt. His head hurt and that made it hard to see or even think. Rising to his feet, Evan stumbled slightly as he made his way to the bathroom. He fingered the clean clothes Everett had left for him.

Everett looked around as he heard shuffling steps behind him, a frown on his face as he watched Evan move towards them and then slide to a sitting position on one of the kitchen chairs his elbows on the table as his hands cradled his head.

"Evan?" Eunice waited for a moment. "Evan?"

"Yeah, Eunice?" He looked up, squinting against the light.

"You're thinking. What about?" Eunice slid a cup of coffee and a plate of toast in front of him. "What happened to you two? Flannery has refused to say. She really didn't even give a statement. Who did they threaten?"

Evan blinked, trying to remember. His head hurt too much, he decided, to even try. He shrugged.

"I have no idea. I don't even remember what happened." He squinted at her again. "What did? And where is Flannery?"

"She's outside somewhere with Lydia." Everett watched his young friend closely, seeing the distress that Evan was trying hard to hide. "She won't talk to us, Evan. That fact alone makes us sure that you were threatened, that we were." Everett twisted his mug in his hands, his eyes on it.

"More than likely." Evan sighed, his head drooping for a moment before he raised it, staring at the outside door. "She's outside?"

"She is. She wanted to be by herself. Lydia found her." Eunice frowned. "It's been too quiet out there, Everett." She was on her feet, her instincts telling her something was wrong.

———

Evan was on his feet, unsteady as he felt, and following her, Everett's hand on his arm to help keep him upright. He stood, a frown in place, before he moved towards the dock, stopping suddenly as he saw the mugs sitting on the chair arms, but no sign of Flannery or Lydia.

"Eunice?" Evan turned to watch her.

Eunice was moving quickly towards the road, her eyes on the ground. Her heart fell as she recognized the tread from her daughter's shoes and the marks from Flannery's crutches. They had disappeared, right from their own yard, and right under her nose. *How did that happen? Lord,* her heart cried, *protect them. Help us to find them.* She didn't hear the sounds of nature around her, missed the squirrels and chipmunks and mice running away from her approach. She paused at the road and then sighed, a deep worried mother's sigh, as she reached for her phone.

Dooley approached Eunice an hour later, a frown on his face.

"No sign of them?"

Eunice shook her head. "The tracks are all I can find. They have disappeared, Dooley." She was a worried mother at that point, her arms wrapping around her waist, not the professional that she normally was.

"We'll find them, Eunice. That's a fact. Now, let's talk with Evan again. See what he has to say." Dooley turned Eunice to walk towards her home.

"He doesn't remember, Dooley. We asked him." She sighed. "And we need him to."

"The concussion would have done that, more than likely. And if he was unconscious for any length of time when they were taken, he wouldn't know what was said."

"I think that's what happened. Flannery refused to talk to us. She was in bed early last night, not just from her pain and fatigue. She's hiding. I think that if she didn't have a cast on her foot, she would have run during the night."

"I suspect that you are correct in that assumption. I can see her wanting to run but not, just because of Evan. He's kept her here."

"That he has." Eunice paused at the door, her hand on the knob before she turned. "How far would they have taken those two? Evan said they had gotten away but he wasn't even sure how they did that or even how far they had managed to get before whatever it was happened. Somehow, I think that they were just dumped on the trail, their captors thinking they would never be found. It's not a trail that is used very often."

"No, it's not." Dooley rubbed at his face, a thought coming up. "We need to backtrack from where we found them. Tag said he'd be around today and would do that."

"Tag? Good. And I know Joe is heading this way again. He called last night, worried about Evan. He muttered something about a hit being contracted on Evan. He just didn't say why."

"A contract? From his street days?" Dooley shook his head, following Eunice into the house. "That's not what I wanted to hear, Eunice."

"What's not, Dooley?" Evan's eyes had cleared somewhat but they could see the pain in his face, the pain just not from his physical injuries, but from his heart hurting for his lady. He missed her greatly, he thought, and struggled to come up with a plan or something, he wasn't quite sure of, in order to find her.

Everett watched Evan closely before he looked up at Eunice, a slight shake of his head at her unspoken question. Evan hadn't given much more information than what they already knew. That concerned Everett. None of them were sure if Evan had remembered something and was hiding it from them, intending to search on his own or if he really didn't remember.

Chapter 38

Tag headed towards Evan, reaching for the mug of coffee extended to him, and then nodding towards the dock. The two men headed that way, Dooley watching Evan closely. Joe stood beside Dooley, his eyes on Eunice.

"No word, Dooley?"

"Not a word, Joe. That's surprising. I would have thought that someone would have put in some kind of demand already." Dooley paused. "We still don't know why Evan and Flannery were taken in the first place. That's the bizarre part of all this." Dooley was more worried than he wanted to let on.

Joe nodded, knowing what Dooley wasn't saying. "It is very strange. There is an undercurrent in all this that just doesn't make sense. We've searched and can't find it. There has to be someone who can do that for us."

Eunice had approached. "There is a firm that we used at one time with the force I was with. Tracker's. I have asked them to look into the names we have. A Jace there promised that he would. Apparently, he knows Evan but won't say how."

"No, I didn't think they would." Joe knew the firm that Eunice was talking about. He knew also that they kept their work as quiet as they were able to. He had talked with Evan about Tracker's in the past, but Evan had been noncommittal with his words, and Joe had had to accept that.

"Jace said he'd forward what he found as he could." Eunice sighed, her heart raising in desperate pleas for her daughter and for her young friend. Her pleas turned to praise and then she prayed for peace. That was what they needed, she knew, peace and confidence in God that He was in control and knew where the young ladies were.

Evan rose eventually, a shuttered look on his face, as he made his way from the cabin, heading towards his own home. Tag paced with him, not saying anything, knowing that his friend would speak when he was able to.

"Tag? Did you find out anything at all?" Evan sank down into his favourite chair, a finger rubbing at his forehead to try and ease the pain.

"I did. I was waiting to talk with you." Tag headed back from the kitchen, mugs of coffee in his hand. He had watched Evan as he had worked in the kitchen preparing their hot drinks and then sandwiches for them both. "We'll eat. Then we pray. Then we talk."

Evan shot him a glance and then nodded. He had been praying continuously, he thought, desperate to have confidence that both Flannery and Lydia would soon be home. Somehow, he didn't think that would happen.

Tag waited for Evan to reach for his sandwich before he shook his head. Evan was not himself, that was obvious. *Lord, You have promised so much. To protect us. I have searched Your Word for those verses, driven to find them. Evan is at a loss right now, dear Lord. Protected his lady and Lydia as well. Give him the peace that he needs.* Tag drew in a deep breath, knowing that the ladies may never come home. That their bodies may never be found. *Dear Lord, not that but if it happens, let us all have the peace that we need, knowing that they would be with you.*

Evan squinted at his friend, setting aside his sandwich before he sighed and reached for it again. Flannery would be after him to eat, challenging him to do just that. *Lord, she has challenged me in so many ways but always in such a way that I grow. She never belittles when she does that. Instead, I can see that her challenge is to make me grow, grow in my love for her and also in my love and walk with You.*

"Tag? You are here for a purpose." Evan had finished his sandwich and sat, his mug of coffee wrapped in one hand.

"I am, Evan. But first, we need to pray and pray hard for your lady."

Evan raised his head at long length, feeling the hand of God on him as he struggled to come to terms with Flannery and Lydia being missing. He frowned, bringing his headache on again. He rubbed at his forehead, Tag watching him closely, then turning as the door opened.

Joe stood for a moment before he headed for the kitchen, returning with a mug of tea, sitting on the hearth and watching the two younger men.

"What conclusion have you two come to?" Joe sipped at his tea, his eyes shifting between Evan and Tag.

"We haven't discussed it yet, Joe. We spent time in prayer." Evan sighed, his eyes closing for a moment. "Do you have any word?"

"No. Dooley said they were trying to track what make of vehicle but hadn't been able to. That makes me think that it's a car or truck that is from the area."

Tag nodded. "I agree. We've tracked the perps to here, now haven't we?" He watched Joe for a moment. "What aren't you saying, Joe?"

Evan's glance shifted to Tag and then to Joe. He frowned for a moment before he spoke.

"I spoke with Jace at Trackers. He's looking into things for me."

"Jace?" Joe shook his head. "I didn't know that you were familiar with him."

"I am." Evan's lips clamped shut. There was no way that he would say how or why he knew Jace. That was a part of his past that he was trying hard to hide and forget. Jace had worked with him on one of his cases, providing names and other data that had helped Evan to find the murderer of a small child and bring him to justice.

"I see." Joe rose and headed for Evan's desk, retrieving pens and pads of paper. "We don't have our whiteboards, fellows, but we can work it almost as one of the detectives would. Now, where do we start?"

Chapter 39

Peering through blurry eyes, Evan rose and headed for the kitchen, turning on lights as he moved that way. Late afternoon was upon them, and he really wasn't sure that they had made any progress. He prayed that they had, a faint hope rising within him. *Lord, please? Protect my lady. Hide her in the hollow of Your hand, in the cleft of the rock and cover her there. Bring Flannery and Lydia back and soon.* Reaching for the kettle, he plugged it in, dumping out the stale coffee and setting the coffee pot to make fresh.

Tag appeared at his side, the bottle of pain medication in his hand.

"Take some, Evan. You can hardly see for that headache."

Evan nodded at long last, taking the tablets he was handed and swallowing them, his throat working to do that.

"Tag? Have we made progress?" Hope was in his voice but he feared that they were no closer than they had been.

"We have, Evan. Don't lose hope. We'll find them. Jace has sent an email to Joe and he's working through it right now. He'll want to print it though."

Evan nodded once more and headed for his computer, pulling up the program that Joe would need and then stepping away, swaying slightly from fatigue. Joe watched him closely before a hand was out lead him to the couch and then gently shove Evan to a sitting position.

"Feet up, Evan. You need to rest for a bit. I'll work through what Jace has sent and he has sent a lot. Then we'll talk after we share a meal and more prayer. We'll find your lady and Lydia. Trust me on that. Dooley and Daniel are working hard. So is Eunice."

"I know, Joe. It just hurts that they are missing. I am afraid that we won't find them in time." Evan frowned again, thinking that he was doing that a lot lately. "I just don't get why Lydia was taken."

"Lydia was with Flannery. She would have seen who was there." Tag shared a long look with Joe. "And then, from what I understand, she has been working to stop the human trafficking and drug trade overseas. We have word that whoever she was fighting against there is the one that is after Flannery."

Evan dozed off and on as Joe and Tag continued to work, their eyes watching him at times before they would share a look. He shouldn't have come home, they thought. He needed medical attention and would just refuse if they tried to force him to go.

"Joe? Did you read this?" Tag's finger paused on a paragraph. "This bit about the Duke?"

"Not yet." Joe flipped through the pages, finding the paragraph that had caught Tag's attention. "The Duke? He's a brother to the Earl?"

"He is. And they are rivals. Not a nice family at all. No brotherly love there. Not from what we've been given." Tag sat back, staring into space. "So, who is actually the one we want to find?"

Evan shifted so that he could watch the two men. "You say they're brothers?" At Tag's nod, he shook his head and regretted it, the headache beginning to pound again. "That's what the word was on the street. Brothers who were rivals. One trying to outdo the other. One worked in this country. The other overseas. But the overseas one was making moves to take over here. Bringing in people and drugs. We could never get a real sense of why or how. Did Jace give anything on that?"

Joe shot him a look before he leafed through the papers in front of him, pausing.

"How did you know?"

"Know what?" Evan was puzzled.

"Jace has confirmed that." Joe's face grew grave. "The country the Earl was working in? That's where Lydia was."

Evan sighed. "I thought that. I knew where she had been but had prayed that she had avoided being found out and identified. I would hazard a guess that the Earl knows her name and where she was and what she was doing. That's likely why she was taken. Flannery knows more than what she has said. I wish she had been upfront and talked with us."

"She's scared, Evan." Tag sat back, his pen tapping gently on the pile of papers that he had been looking through. "She's scared and really not sure who she can trust or if she does trust, how far she can take that trust."

"Tag's right." Joe rose and began to pace. "Now that we know who they are, we need to find them. Did Jace give their names?"

Tag shot him a startled look and then rapidly worked through the papers, pausing with a hand in the air as he read the last one. "He has. He says his boss, Tracker, has confirmed it. As soon as he mentioned the Duke to her, she had given him names of his men, the name for the Earl and who he had working for him. She also said she has a wealth of material that she is sending on to the respective forces. How did she know?"

Evan gave a short laugh. "I've met her, Tag. She has a scary memory. She can connect people from years ago without having to look up any information."

"She can? I'm glad that she is working with us." Joe sat back down, his phone out as it chimed. "It's Eunice. She hasn't found out anything more. She's worried about you, Evan."

"And so she should be. Everett won't say much, but he'll be out there searching for his daughter. That's a given. I just pray that he stays safe." Evan's eyes closed for a moment as he thought through the verses

---

on the protection that he had been reading through over the last few days. He felt strongly that the ladies were in grave danger. But how did they find them? And how did they get them back home and keep them hidden?

Tag stared down at his phone, before he was on his feet, heading for the computer. Retrieving the pages that he had printed, he hurried back to his seat, sorting through them, and then handing a copy to Joe.

"Joe? Here. Jace just sent this." Tag looked over at Evan. "Evan's asleep?"

"I'm not sure if he's sleeping or praying. What's this?" Joe glanced up at Tag, seeing the stress that he was under and prayed for his young friend. "Tag?"

"What? Oh, this. Jace sent it on. He's found more information for us. He's even found a place here that the Earl uses. It's on the lake, but well fortified."

Evan had been listening, his eyes closed and then spoke.

"The old Waters place. It was rumoured to have been sold to someone overseas. That makes horrible sense." He sat up, rubbing at his forehead, the headache somewhat lessened than it had been.

"That's right." Tag sat back. "I'm not real familiar with it."

Evan rose, heading for his bookshelves and retrieving a map.

"Let's lay this out. It's a topographical map of the area. We'll take a look at it and see what we can find."

Tag nodded and then paused.

"One of the map programs on the internet. We might be able to get a visual from the air."

"That's possible." Joe paced through the rooms before he sprung, a finger in the air and his phone out. He moved away to make his call, turning to watch Evan.

"I have someone who can send up a drone and look it over." Joe's words when he returned brought Evan's and Tag's heads up before they looked at him.

"A drone?" Tag shook his head. "Modern technology. I hadn't thought of that."

Joe grinned. "You should have. Now, let's see what we can do."

Chapter 40

Mid-morning the next day, Evan leaned against a tree near the old Waters place. He had sought permission from that homeowner for them to be on his property and was readily granted it. Joe walked towards Tag and himself, a young woman pacing beside him.

"Evan. Tag. This is Joy. She's the one with the drone." He held up a hand as Evan opened his mouth. "It's okay. She's in law enforcement and has done this before. She'll be very careful." He paused, his eyes on the lake that was visible through the trees. "Let's spend some time in prayer, people. We need to bathe this in prayer. If the ladies are there, we need to have proof."

Joy nodded. "That we do, Joe." She waited, her head bowed as she felt the power of the men's prayers, an awakening in her heart. She had hardened her heart years ago, her life as an officer doing that to her. She realized as she listened that she had been wrong and needed to find her way back. "Now, let's head out to the lake. Tag? Joe said you'd take me out and then along the shoreline."

"That I will. I have a canoe here or the homeowner has a rowboat. Which is better?"

Joy bit at her lip for a moment as she thought. "The canoe, I think. We can get undercover better with that, I think. My plan is for us to shelter near the shore on the other side of the property and then I send up the drone. Are you three prepared for this?"

Evan nodded. "We are. We need to find out if Flannery and Lydia are there. That's provided we can see them."

"That's the problem, isn't it?" Joe sighed to himself. "And if they are kept inside, we won't see them."

Tag and Joy headed for the lake and the canoe that Tag had carried down there. Setting out, Tag looked around.

"Where do you want to position yourself, Joy?"

Joy searched the area and then pointed. "Those trees there. They will shelter us, but they're not thick enough to hide the line of sight for me." She bit at her lip for a moment. "Tag? What happened? Joe just said he had a property to search for some missing ladies."

Tag sighed and then spoke, briefly giving a history of what had happened to Evan and Flannery.

"Flannery? I know a young woman about my age with that name. She was on the streets."

"That was likely Flannery. She has not had a home for years, moving from town to town. She's been chased. Evan is trying to help her, but she is not certain who to trust or even how much to trust."

"That happens when they have had to live like that. She helped out a friend of mine who ran into trouble. We looked for her to thank her and to see what we could do for her, but she had disappeared." Joy sighed. "It was around that time that the Duke moved through town. Word on the street was that he was looking for her and it wasn't for the good of her health."

"That's true. He never looks for anyone for their good." Tag didn't say anything more, feeling like Joy was fishing for information. He pointed to the drone. "How long will you need?"

———

"Fifteen or twenty minutes. Maybe a bit longer. There is a camera on it and I'll hand Joe the SD card from it." Joy turned to Tag. "Tag, will you pray once more? This bothers me, that they might be there, and we can't find them."

"We all suspect that will be the case. Just do what you can, Joy. That's all we ask." Tag waited patiently, his eyes on the property, watching the men who appeared to watch the drone. "You're good, Joy."

"Thank you. I belong to a club that flies model airplanes. This is a breeze compared to some of them." She brought the drone back down, her eyes on the men as they walked back into the house. "Now, I can retrieve it and we can head back. Do you think that they saw us?"

"I hope not. Let's wait a few minutes, just in case." Tag took the SD card handed him and tucked it into his shirt pocket, buttoning it close. He ducked his head to watch the property and then reached for the paddle. "I'm heading away from here and away from Joe and Evan and then back towards them. Maybe they won't think it odd."

"I pray not, Tag. We need to find those two ladies." Joy's eyes were in constant movement, searching for anyone who meant them harm. "I think we're okay. We're far enough out that even with binoculars I don't think they can get a good look at us. You're heading farther down the lake and then back towards Joe and Evan?"

"That's my plan. I hope it works."

Joe was at the shore to help pull in the canoe, his eyes watching the lake as he stood upright once more. He shook his head as Tag went to speak and pointed behind him. Tag and Joy shared a look before nodding and moving away from the shore.

Evan watched, a finger rubbing at his forehead. He was still fighting a headache, not as bad as it had been, he thought, but they're enough that it would only ease if he kept still. He headed back towards Tag's truck, knowing that they needed to move away from that area, but he was so reluctant too. He could sense that Flannery and Lydia were both on the property next door.

Joe watched Evan carefully, knowing that the younger man was at his limit but would refuse to give in. He had seen that all too often when Evan was working the streets and then undercover.

"Joe?" Tag paused for a moment, watching as Joy moved up beside Evan. "He's not doing well."

"No, he's not. I heard him up, pacing around the cabin last night. He won't rest until Flannery's back with him unless he collapses."

"And that is exactly what I am afraid of. He still hasn't been able to tell us how they were hurt and on that particular trail. Dooley and Eunice can't figure that out."

"I spoke with Eunice this morning about that. She's at a loss. We need to find her daughter."

The two men shared a look, dread in their hearts for what might well face the two young ladies. Tag just shook his head, heading for his truck.

"Joy? Do you have time to come with us to Evan's?" Joe paused beside her, knowing that her vehicle was parked near his.

"I wish I could, Joe. I have to head back. Duty calls. I need to catch some sleep before I go on tonight." She hesitated for a moment. "Call me if you need any more photos. I can swing that for you." Joy bit at her lip for a moment, a mannerism that Joe recognized as Joy being uncertain. "Thank you for your prayers, you guys. You've directed me back to where I need to be." She was gone before he could say another word, leaving Joe staring after her.

Chapter 41

Hearing a knock at his door a week later, Evan headed for it, rubbing at his temple. His headache had lessened but was still there enough for him to notice. He had spent the week searching for Flannery and Lydia, heading out onto the lake in his canoe, finding a spot to hide and watch the Waters' place. There had been no sign of them. Evan knew that both Everett and Eunice were searching as well. Neither of his friends were sleeping much and that concerned him.

Opening the door, he frowned at the couple standing there, just older than himself, he thought. He sighed to himself. *This is not what he wanted,* he decided. *I want to be out on the lake, overcast and dreary as it was, just in case the ladies were outside. But he doubted that they would be.* He had studied the fence at the back of the guest house as it was called. He wouldn't be able to see them there, even if they were outside.

"Can I help you?" Evan's gaze shifted between the man and woman.

"You're Evan?" At his nod, the man stretched out his hand. "I'm Abe Finlay. This is my wife, Emma. You have been working with Jace. He works for Emma."

"Tracker's?" Evan stood back, motioning them to enter. "Have a seat somewhere. I have to apologize. I've been working through some stuff, trying to find out more than I could." He headed for the kitchen. "You've been travelling. Coffee?"

"For me." Abe shared a look with Emma. "Do you have tea?"

"That I do. I have a selection. I keep it here for Lydia. What kind can I get you, Emma?"

"Apple spice, if you have it. If not, ordinary tea works." Emma paced for a moment before she turned to watch him, her gray eyes thoughtful.

Abe took the mug handed to him and then sat on the couch, Emma beside him, the package that she had been holding dropped on the low table in front of her. Evan sat, his eyes on Abe, wondering just why they had come.

"Evan, I know that we have not met. Can I pray with you before we start talking about why we are here?" Abe waited as Evan hesitated and then nodded, their heads bowing as Abe petitioned God for the safe return of the two ladies and peace for Evan and Lydia's family. He also prayed for direction for the search, knowing by experience just how dangerous it was for the two ladies.

Abe sipped at his coffee, staring past Evan for a moment before his eyes returned to the younger man.

"Evan, let me explain a bit of our history. My father and uncle had set up a security team. They would go in and rescue people as he called it. He also provided security for important people or VIPs as they are called. When I took over and brought in a partner, we changed what we do. We do training now in security with our team of eight, including Murphy and me. We still will go in and find people and bring them out safely. Emma and I had an adventure, which we will tell you later. But for now, Emma has information that she needs to share with you. She has sent it on to Joe and Tag as well. Eunice has been provided with it. She was quite taken aback that Emma had reached out to her."

"She would be, but she and Everett would be so thankful. God bless you both." Evan twisted the mug sitting on the table beside him, not quite sure what to expect. His eyes turned to Emma, seeing the compassion on her face. "Emma?"

"Evan, I know Tag has provided you with what Jace had given you. I am stepping in where I normally don't. If Jace has been the one finding the information, he should be the one speaking with you. But he is unable to come to talk with you and asked that I do. He felt it best given the men that you are looking at."

"The Duke and the Earl?" Evan shook his head. "How did they get those names?"

Emma gave a grim smile. "It goes back to their father. He was a king in the drug trade years ago. The men who worked for him were nicknamed the sons. They are twins, by the way. When their father was killed by a rival drug lord, they fought each other to take over his empire. A nasty bit of work they are. The Duke won and the Earl left that area. The Waters' place? That is hidden behind multiple names. That no one would have known if they hadn't known the history of the Waters. They are related to the two men, cousins in fact. The Earl took over their property and chased them away. We have been unable to determine exactly where they are."

"They would be dead, more than likely, and their bodies buried somewhere." Evan paled somewhat. "There are lots of places there that they could be. There have been rumours for years about people being buried. The kids would try and go on the property to find the ghosts."

Abe gave a quick grin. "That they would, and they would not have gotten too far. He has security on there all the time."

"Security? That explains it. We thought that but had nothing to confirm it." Evan turned back to Emma. "Okay. So, what else?"

Emma reached to hand him the package. "In here is all the information Jace and I have been able to find. A lot of it was hidden but we've managed to do just that." She shook her head at him questioning look. "I'm sorry, Evan. I can't explain how we do it. We have programs that we run searches with. That helps. But I can remember people and connections that I can't explain."

Evan paged through the papers, reaching for a pen and then a highlighter. Emma watched him closely. Abe had risen and headed outside, concern on his face for his new friend. He nodded as he searched the outside. *Evan's good,* he thought. *Joseph will be happy to hear that he has good security.* He turned as he heard footsteps approaching.

Eunice and Everett paused for a moment before they walked towards Abe, her hand tight in her husband's.

"Hi! You're here to see Evan?" Eunice tilted her head to study Abe. "I think that we have met."

"I'm Abe Finlay. My wife, Emma, is in the cabin, going over material with Evan. You're Eunice and Everett, Lydia's parents."

"That we are." Eunice shared a look with Everett. "What has Emma done?"

"You know her, I gather. She has found a wealth of information. It has gone to the force here and then to Joe and also Tag, at Jace's request." Abe pointed to the door. "We want to do what we can to help bring the ladies home. My team is ready to move in, if and when they are asked."

Everett was confused and it showed on his face. "I don't understand. Your team?"

Abe grinned. "I have a security team. We do training now but we used to go in and bring people out of situations that they found themselves in. We still do it but are selective as to who we work with." He nodded at the door. "I know Evan's father. I can't say why, but when Jace saw the name and mentioned it to Emma, she recognized it." He held up a hand as he laughed. "And don't ask how she remembers names and events and makes connections. She just can't explain it other than it's God working through her."

"And He does that. Thank you, Abe." Eunice headed for the door and disappeared through it.

Everett watched her go. "What didn't you say, Abe?"

Abe nodded. Everett is good, he thought, considering he's not former law enforcement.

"We've had a word about Flannery. We're not sure what all is planned for her, but it likely will lead to her death. She knows something that she has forgotten or has hidden deep in her memory. And if she remembers, that could be tragic for her."

Chapter 42

Pacing around the outside of his cabin as dusk was falling that night, Evan's thoughts were troubled. He had heard what Emma had to say, had read and reread the material that she had provided for him, and his thoughts were still muddled. *What did she do, Lord? What does my Flannery know that she hasn't shared? Protect her, Lord. Bring her home to us.*

Walking towards the dock that stretched out into the lake, Evan paused as he stood beside a chair before he sank down. His head lowered, he sat and listened to the night sounds awakening and the day sounds quietening. He needed this solitude, to spend time in the presence of his Lord and just to listen and be refreshed. *Lord, still my heart, please. Help me to listen to Your voice in the stillness of the night. Lord, please bring my lady home. Bring Lydia back. But I know I have to be willing to accept that they don't come home or if they do, it's a funeral that we have, not a joyous reunion.*

Evan repeated this sitting in the silence before God every night for the next week. His heart would grow quiet, and he began to feel the peace that God was providing for him. He still searched every day but was also involved in deciding what he wanted to do. Evan knew that he had no desire to return to policing. He had been beaten up on the streets and knew his heart was no longer in that. Just what was it that he wanted to do? That he wasn't even sure of anymore. Joe had talked at length with him as had Everett. Evan valued their counsel but even at that, he was still troubled. He just knew he wanted to live in the cabin where he had spent so much time with his father.

Eight days after the ladies had disappeared, Evan walked quickly along the path towards Eunice and Everett's. Sam met him partway there and Evan dropped to his knees to wrap the dog in his arms, a few tears soaking in the dog's heavy coat.

"You miss them, don't you, Sammy?" A low woof greeted his words. "We need to find them. I just feel as if today is the crucial day. What if we don't find them, we won't."

Everett watched as Evan stood and then walked towards him.

"Evan?"

"Everett, have you heard anything?"

Everett shook his head. "Not a thing. I did hear from that Abe. He's heading this way, he said. Just didn't say why."

"No, he won't. Not until or unless he has to. That's how he is. We had a good talk when he was here a week ago." Evan paused as he saw Eunice just standing and staring at the chairs. He knew that she was worried, much more than someone who was not in law enforcement. They knew and saw too much, that he knew.

"How is she?" Evan nodded towards Eunice.

"She's hanging in there. She just wants Lydia home. This is worse than when she was overseas. At least then we had contact and knew where she was." Everett drew in a deep breath, his eyes troubled as he stared at the hands that he was rubbing together. "We've talked, Evan. We have both had to release her to God, to be able to say what He wills. If she comes home or not, we have to be prepared for both events."

"I know. I have had to do the same." Evan groaned as he felt his phone vibrating. "This thing has been going crazy today. No one is there when I answer, and no text messages are coming through." He stared down at the phone. "Tag is on his way here as is Joe."

"What happened with the pictures that Joy took? Did they show anything?" Everett had not heard but was hopeful that something had.

"Not really. There is a high fence around the guest cottage. That's new, within the last month or so, we think."

Everett paled under his tan. "New? This was planned." Everett spun and walked away, heading for Eunice before he was back beside Evan, a hand on his arm. "Did they plan this? Did they follow Lydia as well?"

Evan paused, biting at his lower lip before he nodded.

"That's what we are hearing now. Someone has come forward with that. Joe said they're working on it but it doesn't help find the ladies or get them home."

Everett dropped his head, working to control his emotions. *That was not what he had needed to hear,* he thought, before he began to pray hard for his daughter and the young lady who had wiggled her way into their family and hearts. Flannery had become just like another daughter to them.

Hearing the sound of a vehicle nearing his cabin, Evan excused himself and walked away, not seeing Everett standing with his hand on Sam's head, watching. Everett sighed to himself before he turned and walked back towards Eunice, reaching to wrap her in his arms. Their fear for their daughter had grown each day. They were just so afraid that she would never return to them, that she would just disappear, and they would never know if she was still alive or dead.

Evan stared at the two large black SUVs that parked behind his vehicle and then his brow cleared as Abe walked towards him.

"Evan?"

"Abe." Evan watched as seven men milled around the vehicles. "What is going on?"

"Can we go inside? All of us? We need to talk." Abe followed him inside, hearing the footsteps of his team as they followed suit.

Abe walked through to the kitchen, reaching for the coffee pot.

"Can we, Evan? We're going to need this. We have information that we need to go over with you. We are here for the only reason to find Flannery and Lydia and bring them home. That happens today."

Evan stared at him, hope beginning to rise in his heart.

"You know where they are?"

"We do." Murphy, Abe's partner, spoke from beside Evan. "They are close to here, but not where they had been." He shook his head at the look on Evan's face. "We have received word that they have been moved. Emma has confirmed it. And don't ask how she has. She can't explain it."

"That is what she said." Evan turned to study the door. "Do we need to find Everett and Eunice?"

Abe and the other seven men exchanged glances, knowing what they were facing.

"Not yet, Evan." Abe's hand on his shoulder stopped his forward step. "We need to confirm that the ladies are where we think. What we need from you is your knowledge of the lake and some islands on it."

Evan froze, his hand stopped in the motion of rubbing at his cheek. He paled, knowing what Abe was asking.

"They are on an island? And there is a bad storm system moving in." His eyes slid closed as he groaned. "They're on one of the islands that flood, aren't they?"

Abe sighed to himself. Evan had gone right to the heart of the matter.

"They are. One is called Elm Island. How far out in the lake is it?"

"Not that far. I can see it from here. But so can anyone at the Waters." Evan began to pace, moving among the eight men.

Murphy stopped beside Abe.

"He'll want to go with us."

"I know. And we can't let him. Tag said he'd leave canoes for us to use. I don't think Evan knows that."

"No, I don't think he would. Now, we just have to keep him here."

"That's where Joseph comes in. He's staying with Evan. Nathaniel will be onshore, keeping watch. Tag left two canoes and said Evan had one as well." Abe turned away to reach for his mug of coffee, knowing that their plans were in place. They just had to wait for twilight.

Chapter 43

Twilight found Abe, Murphy, and the other four of their team, Luke, Ian, Micah, and Matt, heading for the lake. They set off for the island that they could only barely see. Joseph had stopped Evan from moving towards the shore, simply shaking his head.

"We need you to stay inside, Evan. If you are down there, it may give away what we are up to. Don't worry. They'll be fine. We've done this before."

"What? Cross a lake when a storm brewing?"

Joseph grinned. "You don't want to know the conditions that we have had to work in. Now that we are all married and with children, we are glad that we don't have to travel."

"I guess that would make a big difference." Evan sank down into a chair in the living room, his eyes on the fire that had been lit in the fireplace. "How do you do it,

Joseph? How do you trust that much in God to keep you safe?"

Joseph shrugged. "It's called faith, Evan. Our faith in God has deepened over the years. It has to have. You either grow or run. We chose to grow in God. He has us in His hands. If He chose to take us home while we were out on a mission, we accepted that." He looked up as he heard the wind picking up, praying hard for his teammates. It was dangerous, he knew, what they were attempting. But they had all been in agreement. They had to make that attempt.

Abe drew up the canoe that he had been in and waited for the other men to follow suit. He pointed to the island and then to each man. They nodded, familiar with what they needed to do. Creeping forward, keeping to the shadows, they approached the decrepit cabin. Murphy shook his head. There was no way that this cabin would last long. They could all heard the groaning of the logs as the wind picked up.

They crept in cautiously, not able to see well in the darkness. Abe pulled out the small flashlight that he uses in these situations and shone it around, bringing it back as Ian made an exclamation. Matt, the paramedic on the team, sprang forward to drop to his knees beside the ladies. They didn't move as he reached to check for pulses, nodding at Abe's low-spoken question. Flannery and Lydia were quickly gathered into strong arms and the men moved as rapidly as they could back to the canoes. Luke took a look at the sky.

"We need to move fast, Abe. That storm is moving in."

Abe nodded. "I know. Pray that we make it."

Fighting the worsening wind, the men headed back across the lake, fingers white on the paddles. Matt kept an eye on Flannery, who was in the canoe with himself and Luke. He was afraid for her, afraid that they had found the ladies too late. Lydia has roused to some extent when Matt had checked her out but Flannery had made no such movement.

Nathaniel was there to help them pull the canoes well up out of the water, knowing by the looks on his friends' faces just how difficult it had been.

"How are they?" Nathaniel kept his eyes on Abe, knowing the other men were heading for the cabin.

———

"Lydia roused. Flannery hasn't. Matt will look them over." Abe paused, thankful that they had made it safely back. "Listen. I need you and Murphy to head over to Eunice and Everett and bring them over. We can't let them know until they are here that we have the two ladies."

"Sure. Joseph found me. Joe and Tag are here."

"They are? They would be. Okay. Thanks for the heads up." Abe tapped Nathaniel's shoulder as they separated, Nathaniel heading for the trail to the other cabin.

Abe stopped inside the door, watching as Matt worked on Flannery. He could tell by his movements the deep concern that he had. Joe stopped beside him, his own eyes on Evan, who stood as close as he was allowed to Flannery, Tag's arm around his shoulders in support.

"Abe? Where did you find them?"

"On one of the islands. We'll need to speak with whichever officer has been working on this here."

"That's Dooley. Eunice has been involved to a certain extent but stepped back when Lydia disappeared."

"That's only appropriate." Abe moved towards Matt as he stood and looked around for him. "Matt. Talk to me."

"She's in rough shape, Abe. She really should be in a hospital, but I don't know if that would be a wise move."

"Not likely at present. Go and get your kit. Do what you can for her. Everett's a retired paramedic so he'll be involved."

"That he will." Matt walked rapidly from the room.

Evan moved closer, his hand resting on Flannery's hair, a prayer raised in praise that the Lord had protected her, had hidden her in the cleft of the rock and saved her life. Only now that she was home, he didn't know if she would survive. He could read the look on Matt's and Abe's faces and feared the worse.

"Abe?"

"Evan, she's alive. Matt will do what he can. We don't want to take them to the hospital if we can avoid it."

Evan nodded. "And the weather is starting to get bad. Severe thunderstorms are expected. They are always bad here. We could ask Doc Benson to come out but it's too risky right now. He's not that young, either."

"I see. Matt will do what he can." Abe turned slightly to watch his teammates and then his eyes dropped to Lydia. "He's taken a look at Lydia. She came off better than Flannery."

"I suspected that she would. It's been a long week, eight days, whatever it has been. I can only praise God that they are here. Everett and Eunice?"

"Nathaniel headed to find them."

"Eunice was on duty tonight. Everett should be home. And Sam."

"Sam?" Murphy frowned as he stared at Evan.

"Everett's dog. He's claimed Flannery. If he comes, you won't get close to her."

Chapter 44

Everett came to an abrupt halt as he entered Evan's cabin, Nathaniel closing the door behind them. Sam moved through the room, finding Lydia, his head resting on her leg as he stared at her. Looking at Abe as he approached, Everett froze, his face feeling tight and tense.

"Abe? You're here? Nathaniel said your whole team was here. But he didn't say why you wanted me here."

"Everett. We have your daughter." Abe watched with compassion as Everett took a moment to understand his words before his eyes slid closed and tears appeared on his cheeks. "We have her."

Everett watched as the men moved so that he could see his daughter. A stifled sob sounded in the room before he was across it to kneel at his daughter's side, a shaking hand on her hair. The men could see his lips moving but the words were inaudible. He looked up after a moment.

"Flannery?"

"She's here. Matt is working on her." Abe moved away, to step outside, Joe with him. "We need to find Eunice."

"Already done. I spoke with the desk officer. He's finding a replacement for her and sending her home. I'll go meet her."

"Thank you, Joe. We can stay until tomorrow. It doesn't look as if it will be wise to travel."

"Not likely. This storm is really moving in. If you had been any later heading out, you wouldn't have made it. I know the island from Evan. It will flood, completely covering it. Storms like this one? Two to three feet. These two would not have survived." He looked around as the door opened and Evan appeared.

"Abe? How can we thank you?" Evan didn't know there were tear tracks on his cheeks.

"No thanks are necessary, Evan. It's what we do and who we are." Abe hesitated for a moment. "You'll have to call it in."

"I know. I have." He stared down at his phone, rubbing a thumb along the edge of it. "Dooley's on his way out. He came in to work for Eunice. Eunice?"

"Joe's heading that way to find her. We'll stay until tomorrow, Evan, and give what we can to Dooley. There are things that we will not tell him. We can't."

"We understand that." Evan turned to stare at the door. "How long would they have been there?"

"The word we received was that it was last night when they were left there. Why?"

Evan shrugged. "I thought I heard a motorboat late last night, which is odd. No one boats at night on this lake."

"That was likely them." Abe watched as Joe walked away. "We'll find help for them, Evan. They'll need someone to talk to."

"They will need that." Evan moved back from the front of the porch, feeling the rain starting. "The storm is here. Pray that we avoid the tornado that they warned about."

"We have been." Abe's hand rested on Evan's shoulder. "Evan, let me pray with you. I know you have been trusting, as tough as it has been, for God to work and bring the ladies home. He has done that. Now, we need to get them well. That will be hard on you. You will want to help them. They will reject it, but not reject you. Keep in mind that mind games will have been played with them. That is something God will heal. They won't be the same though as they were before."

Evan nodded. "I saw it, Abe. I saw it on the streets. I hate that this happened to them."

"We both have seen too much, Evan. But the paths that God has led us on have prepared us for this. You will need to watch Flannery closely. She'll try and run if she can, just to protect you and in doing so protect her heart. I sense that you have feelings for her. Just continue as you have and surround her with prayer. The same for Lydia." Abe squinted through the darkness. "And there is Joe and Eunice. And that must be Dooley arriving as well."

Eunice stopped for a moment, staring at Abe before she turned to Evan, hugging him tightly.

"Joe said the girls are here?"

"They are, Eunice. Abe and his men found them and brought them home. Dooley's here to talk to Abe. He'll have to wait, though, to speak with Flannery and Lydia."

Eunice nodded before she was through the door, finding Everett waiting for her to wrap her in his arms. The tears started as she moved away to kneel by her daughter, arm around her, her hand on her hair. Everett walked away, his emotions overcoming him for a moment. He stepped out the back door and tucked himself into a corner, watching the trees bending in the strong winds. Ian stood and watched him, shaking his head. He could not imagine how he felt.

Chapter 45

Lydia roused the next morning, feeling warm and taken care of. She refused to open her eyes, listening to the quiet footsteps and soft voices. She sensed someone near her and felt a hand on her head.

"Lydia? Can you wake up, dear?" Eunice had knelt beside her daughter, watching her closely.

Lydia's eyes cracked open, and she frowned at Eunice.

"Mom? Oh, no! You're a captive too!"

"Not at all, dear. You're free. You were brought to Evan's cabin last night. Can you sit up for me? I really need you to drink this juice. Doc's on his way out as well, just to look you over."

Lydia finally managed to sit upright, her mother's arm around her, her father perched on the couch arm. She stared around, seeing Evan and Joe near the other couch.

"Flannery? Is she safe? She was hurt yesterday, no the day before. I don't know how, but she was unconscious when they moved us."

"Matt, a friend and paramedic, looked her over as did your Dad. Doc will assess her." Eunice took the glass from her daughter, noting that she had finished the juice. "Once Doc has seen to you, you'll want to freshen up. Dad went and brought clothes back for both you and Flannery."

Lydia nodded, before she rose, heading away from her parents and hitting the back door. Tag followed her, not willing to let her be outside on her own.

"What? Shouldn't I have come outside?" Lydia felt belligerent.

"Not likely, but you need to. Just stay back near the wall. It's sheltered." Tag studied her. "What happened, Lydia? What did they say to you?"

Lydia wrapped her arms around herself, shaking in her fear.

"They tried to kill us, Tag. They left us there on the island. Flannery was unconscious. I don't know what they did to her, but they did something. They just dumped us there, Tag. Just dumped us like so much garbage." Lydia blinked back the tears.

"I know they did. It is what they do. We see it. You saw it overseas." Tag had taken a guess.

"I did. I prayed it would never happen to me or a friend. It did. Where is God, Tag? Did He abandon us?"

"Not at all, Lydia. He was there. He kept you through this. You are alive because that it is His will for you."

Lydia had turned to watch him, a shadow in her eyes. Tag sighed. What did they say to you, Lydia, that you aren't ready to tell us?

"Who all did they threaten?"

Lydia began to shake her head and then sighed. "You know them, Tag. Everyone they could think of? That's who they threatened." She frowned, a puzzled look on her face. "They know Evan is here. They want him. They tried to make Flannery agree to make him meet her."

"And she refused. When was that?"

Lydia sighed before she spoke once more. "Yesterday morning. No, the morning before. That's when they pulled her from where they had us locked up. She didn't come back. Instead, they took me out to the boat and she was there. She wasn't moving. What did they do?" Lydia brushed by Tag, almost running to find out what Doc said about her friend.

Doc Benson studied Lydia for a moment and shook his head. She looked okay, he decided, but he knew that she wouldn't be. Who knew what had happened to them over the time that they were gone. They needed to speak about it, but he knew Lydia, or at least he thought he did. She wouldn't unless she was forced to. That was where Dooley came in, he decided.

Doc pulled a chair beside Flannery, watching her closely. He frowned. She was still unconscious, or so he thought. Everett stood near him, Evan as close as he could get.

"Doc? She hasn't woken yet since the team brought her here. She seemed to rouse but not fully." Everett watched her face, a frown in place. "She is tender over the abdomen. Lydia didn't know much of what happened."

"She didn't? Separated them, did they? Let's have a look." Doc worked away on his assessment, knowing that Everett had pulled Evan away. Eunice stood beside him, ready to help in any way.

"Doc? Do we need to take her in?" Eunice kept her voice low.

Doc shook his head. "No, not at present. If we can get her to awaken, then we can do a proper assessment. It looks as if she wasn't eating much, if at all." He turned on his chair to look at Lydia. "Lydia? Was Flannery eating?"

Lydia shook her head. "She refused. For some reason, she just refused. She couldn't or wouldn't tell me why. There was fresh food all the time. They made sure of that." Lydia's brow wrinkled as she thought through their captivity. "She would only drink water from the tap. I had juice and coffee, but she was adamant that she wouldn't touch anything like that. Is that what happened to her, Doc?"

"Part of it likely. They kept you separated two days ago?" Dooley spoke up.

"They did, Dooley. The man came and pulled her out of the cabin just before lunch. She didn't come back. They made me leave around four, I think it was. Why?"

"We need to know if she had anything to eat or drink. Doc needs to know what to do for her. This helps." Dooley shared a look with Evan, who nodded. Dooley frowned at the whiteness of Evan's face. He's not well and now this is added to his worry, he thought.

Doc reached for the IV that Matt had started before he left that morning, nodding. He had been told that a paramedic had been there and treated her as best he could. He had to be at his own practice shortly, he knew, but Everett would be able to help.

"Everett, I'll leave supplies for you. We'll need to keep Flannery on the IVs for now. I have to be back in town. Call me if you are concerned at all. We may need to take her in and have some imaging studies done"

Chapter 46

It was late afternoon before Flannery began to stir and rouse. Evan was on his knees beside her, reaching to touch her face. A whispered prayer reached Flannery's ears and she frowned. Evan? Was he a captive too? There was no way that they were free.

Cautiously opening her eyes, Flannery stared at him and then around the room. Her eyes slid closed. She was free but was Lydia as well? Her hand reached to touch Evan's, bringing his eyes open and to her face.

"Flannery? Oh, thank God! You're awake!" Evan's voice, though low, reached the other in the room and they rose to stare at Flannery. Lydia was beside her, reaching to hug her friend.

"Evan? Where? What happened? Where are they?" Flannery jerked upright, searching the room for their kidnappers.

Her fear, no, terror, Evan thought, was palpable.

"They're not here, Flannery love. You're safe. Abe and his team went in and found you." Evan repeated himself before she looked at him. He drew in a deep breath at the terror in her eyes. "Flannery? What did they do to you?"

Flannery shook her head, her eyes on Joe. "Please, Evan? I need up." She shoved at the blanket covering her and rose, heading for the bathroom, her steps unsteady.

Evan stood and watched her, wanting to help her but knowing that he couldn't. Not yet, at any rate. That he determined to change as soon as he could. He knew without a shadow of a doubt that Flannery was his heart, the part that he was missing. *God, please? Heal my lady. Bring peace back to her.*

Joe watched closely before he moved to stand beside Evan, a hand resting on his shoulder. Everett stood, his arm around Lydia, his gaze shifting between Evan and the closed bathroom door. Lydia moved away, to tap at the door and then slipping through it. The men could hear murmurs from there and then looked at each other.

Everett shook his head and moved away, his heart breaking for the two ladies, before he reached for the soup and tea that he had ready for them.

"Evan? Here. Can we set up to eat in the living room?" Joe was determined to distract Evan, knowing that Dooley would be needed to take Flannery's statement and he just wasn't sure if Evan would step back enough for that to be done.

Lydia stared at Flannery, who was rubbing at her wet hair with a towel. She wasn't quite sure what Flannery was up to. These two young ladies had gotten to know one another over the course of their captivity and had become fast friends.

"You can't run, Flannery. If you do, I'm going with you. We have to stick together." Lydia's voice was low. "That's what they want you to do. If you run, then Evan will come after you. How did they connect you two?"

Flannery lifted her head, staring at Lydia. A thought crossed her mind and her eyes slid closed.

"I saw Evan when he was undercover. He was being watched. I don't know if they knew he was in law enforcement or not. I heard that he had been working to bring down someone named Blackmore.”

“You did? You need to talk to him.” Lydia reached to hug Flannery, praying for them both.

“Lydia? Did you think that we would ever get free?” Flannery rubbed at the counter and didn’t look up.

Lydia leaned back against the wall, her eyes on the tiled floor and the soft yellow rugs that Evan had placed there.

“I prayed that we would. I didn’t know though if we would.” Her words paused as she turned her head to listen. “Dooley’s here, Flannery. You have to tell him what all happened. Please? If you don’t, they will never catch the men who held us.”

“I know. When I was away from you, I heard talk. The Duke and the Earl are really angry with someone. I couldn’t get a sense of who. And they are fighting with one another.” Flannery looked up once more to the ceiling, biting at her lips, blinking to prevent the tears from falling. “They talked about your parents, Lydia.”

“They did? Flannery!” Lydia pulled open the door and pulled Flannery with her.

———

"Dooley? Here's Flannery. She needs to speak with you."

Dooley nodded, watching Flannery carefully. *She's ready to run but doesn't want to.* Evan moved towards her, a hand outstretched that she stared at before she reached for his, letting him lead her to the couch and then seating her before he sat beside her.

"Flannery? Let's eat. Then we talk. And talk we will. And there will be no running away on your part." Dooley was stern but they could see the compassion he felt in his eyes.

Flannery nodded, knowing that she did have to talk, even though she didn't want to. She avoided the eyes of the others in the room, not wanting to see censure. A tray appeared in her vision, startling her before she took it with a quiet word of thanks.

Everett watched her closely, knowing how fragile she was. He sighed as he watched Evan, trying his best to let her know that she was safe but knowing that until the men were caught, no one was safe. He had had a good talk with Abe and Murphy the night before and knew what would likely happen. He feared for their

lives, knowing that the men would come
after the girls and Evan and likely anyone
who got in their way.

Chapter 47

Dooley finally reached for his laptop, knowing that Flannery would want to delay giving her statement, but he had to get it now that she was awake. He looked up to find her watching him and then shifting her gaze to Joe. He frowned. What was up? Dooley knew by experience something was going on.

Flannery stared at Dooley, feeling Evan's arm around her. She sighed. She wanted him to stay away from her. Evan had been threatened and she just didn't know how to tell him that. He had her heart, she knew, and when she walked away, it would break her heart to do so.

"Flannery? Okay. I have to ask the others to leave until we're done. You understand?" Dooley smiled at her brief nod before he watched the other three leave the room to gather on the back porch. "Okay. Let's get you started. And before you even think of running, don't. Evan will come after you. He's been threatened, that much I know, and you will try to protect him. Only you won't be able to. We need to find these men. I can tell you that we're close."

"You are? Okay, then. Can we get started?" Flannery rubbed at her face as she watched Dooley.

"We're set. Let's start. If I have questions, I'll ask them at the end of it all." Dooley prayed for his young friend, knowing just how difficult it was for her.

"Okay. I have to go back to when Lydia and I were taken from her home. They stuffed us into a car and just drove off. I think Lydia knew where we were heading." Flannery's thoughts drifted back to that day.

Both Lydia and she had searched the cabin they were shoved into, trying to find a way out. They searched for weapons, not finding any. Even the sharp knives had been removed. The refrigerator was full of food, which puzzled them.

They had walked out into the backyard, staring up at the high fence, Lydia commenting that there was no way they could climb it, not with Flannery in a cast.

The two ladies had searched for something to keep them occupied, the choice of books and magazines not to their liking. There had been board games and puzzles in plenty. They had stared at one another, realizing that at one time this had been a family home.

"The Waters had six kids." Lydia had paced the living room four days after their captivity started. She suddenly spun, shock on her face. Her finger on her lips, she had reached for a pad of paper and a pen, quickly scrawling out some names.

Flannery took it, staring at Lydia and then at the paper. Her face had whitened as she recognized them. She reached for the pen, quickly looking around, not sure if they were being watched or listened to. She added the Duke and the Earl to the list, a question on her face as she looked up.

Lydia had nodded and leaned close to whisper.

"I think they are related to the Waters. Cousins or nephews, I think. If they are who I think they are, then there was a falling out between the brothers. The younger brother inherited this place."

"Then we know who they are. How do we prove it? And how do we get away?"

Flannery quickly ripped up the piece of paper and stuffed it into the wood stove, not wanting it to be found. She knew she would never forget the names and didn't think Lydia would either.

Three days later, the entry door had flown open, startling the two ladies who spun from where they stood in the kitchen. The large heavyset captor strode across the floor, a hand out to grasp Flannery's arm. She struggled to escape from him, hearing Lydia's cries for her to be left alone. She didn't know that Lydia had flown to the closed and locked door, trying her best to open it and wasn't able to.

Flannery was marched across the lawn and into the main cabin, shoved down into a chair in the office. The man stood beside her, just waiting. She didn't look up as she heard other footsteps approaching.

"Where is he, Flannery?" The voice was coarse, showing the lifestyle of the man who faced her.

Flannery refused to answer, not sure who he was looking for. The questioning continued, the same question asked in different ways. She finally looked up, staring at the man in front of her. She drew in a deep breath. It was him, she thought.

The man who had appeared one day in a different town and then followed her from town to city to village.

"I don't know who you mean. I don't know." Flannery's breath caught in her throat. *This is it, isn't it, Lord? Don't let my friends grieve too much.* She had caught the look of death in the man's glance and knew that she would not survive. She pleaded with God to spare Lydia and then Evan and Lydia's parents.

Her arm grasped tightly, Flannery was hauled to her feet and pulled towards the outside door. She twisted, breaking the grip and running for the outside. She tripped over a box sitting near the door and flew forward, landing heavily on a stump near the bottom of the stairs. The pain hit her in the abdomen before her head hit solidly on the pavement and she dropped into that well of unconsciousness that she had wanted to avoid.

The Earl stood over her, rage sparking from him. He spun to the man with him.

"That island. The one that floods. Take her there. That other thing too. No one will find them." He didn't see his recent hire watching closely before he walked away, to the shadow of the trees and pulling out a phone.

Lydia shook her head in fear and denial as she was approached, moving backwards in the room until she could not move any further. She was dragged from the cabin, her feet digging into the ground, twisting her arm to try and escape. Shoved into a boat, her cries could be heard over the sound of the motor as she reached for Flannery, pulled backwards from that. Sobs rose within her that she tried to quell, her eyes on her friend, lying so still and almost deathlike, she thought.

Approaching an island, the motor was shut off and Lydia was hauled to her feet. Fear grew within her as she recognized the island and then the clouds moving in caught her attention. *Lord, please? Don't let us die. Not here. Not now.* She was shoved ashore and then Flannery was carried up to the ramshackle cabin and dropped roughly before the men headed back to the boat, ignoring Lydia's pleas not to leave them there.

Lydia stood and watched the boat leave, tears on her face, the wind worsening around her. She moved towards the cabin, her eyes searching the lake for anyone that could or would be able to rescue them and seeing no one. She slumped to the floor beside her unconscious friend, knowing that unless they were found, this would be where they died. And just why would God allow that?

Neither lady heard the worsening weather over the next hours nor the darkening sky with the storms moving in. Afterwards, Lydia could not say when she slept but it was at some point. She roused briefly as she was gathered into strong male arms and carried down to the canoe, her voice rough from fear, begging them to help her and to help Flannery. Neither Lydia nor Flannery roused as they were carried from the canoes and into Evan's cabin.

Chapter 48

Dooley tidied away his papers before he looked up at Flannery, seeing the whiteness of her face. He paused, praying for his young friend. He would need to find someone that both she and Lydia could speak, someone who could understand and help them. He knew of a lady and would approach her.

Flannery looked up from her hands that she had been twisting together, drawing in a deep breath.

"Dooley? Those names? Does that help?"

Dooley smiled at the hope in her voice. "They do. You have been able to identify the Earl. Now we need to keep you safe. He'll be after you, you know."

"I know. He'll be hurt." Flannery's eyes flew to the door as she heard Evan's shout, Lydia's scream, and then Everett's voice.

Dooley was on his feet, reaching for his weapon as the door flew open. Evan was shoved violently forward, to land at Flannery's feet and lie still. Lydia was shoved towards a chair and forced to sit. Everett was dragged in and dropped to the floor.

Dooley's hands raised as he was approached, and his weapon removed and dropped on the table behind him. He narrowed his eyes as he stared at the men in front of him and nodded. The Duke had arrived and then he saw the Earl coming in behind his brother.

"So, you two are together. Family feud over?" Dooley's voice held contempt for the men.

"No, it's not. There never was a family feud. That was a front that we put up in order to expand what Daddy had stared." The Duke sneered at him. His eyes turned to Flannery. "Now, this woman? She's coming with us. She knows too much."

Flannery stared at him before her mouth snapped closed. She shook in fear before she felt God moving in her heart and peace enveloped her. She shook her head.

"That's not happening, Victor Waters. Not at all." She looked past him, seeing movement outside the door and frowned before her brow cleared. "I have no idea what you are talking about. I know that you have followed me for months, if not years. Why? I have nothing that you want. I saw nothing."

"But you did." The Duke frowned in turn. "Walter said you did. In Freedom. He said you saw a man killed and he was there watching."

"Sorry. I have never been there. Not in my life. Although maybe I should have been." Flannery caught the faint movement that Evan had made and knew that he was alert again. *Please, just stay put,* she thought. *Lord, help us to get out of this, please? I know. It may be when we die, but You are here. I can feel you.* She frowned again as she watched the movement at the door and saw Joe, Daniel, Tag, and Eunice step quietly in behind the four men.

Dooley waited patiently, his eyes not moving from the Earl. He was the more dangerous of the two, he thought. He caught a movement from one of the men, a younger man, who gave a brief nod at him. Undercover, Dooley thought. Good. That leaves only three of them to take down.

Now to manage that without anyone being hurt.

Daniel moved forward, his weapon jabbing into the Earl's back, who stiffened with that before he started to turn.

"Just stay still, Waters. This is over. We have you now. You are under arrest."

The Earl sneered. "You are outnumbered. It's just you and that man over there."

Daniel gave a brief bark of laughter. "I don't think so. There are four of us behind you, all law enforcement and all armed. And one in front of you. It's over, Waters, for both of you."

The Earl felt the handcuffs as they snapped on his wrist and struggled to escape, unable to avoid the cold steel that now bound him in a way that he had had many others bound. He was pulled from the room, his brother following, as well as the two men with them. Dooley moved to the doorway to watch, Eunice beside him.

"This is it, Dooley?" Hope was in her voice.

"I would suspect so, Eunice. We have underlings to find if we can. They'll scatter once they know their boss is in jail. And he will be there for many years. I spoke with the judge earlier, getting a sense of what we could expect."

"Thank you, Dooley." Eunice turned back to the door. "I'm off duty now. I'll go in and help later but right now, I need to spend time with my family."

"That you do, Eunice. I'll head in and help sort out what is going on. Watch Evan. He was mistreated again." Dooley stepped to where he could see through the door, a smile crossing his face. "Although it looks as if Flannery has that well in hand."

Flannery had dropped to her knees once the men had been removed and touched Evan's back. Evan moved, pain in his movements before he rolled over, a hand raising to Flannery's face.

"You're okay, sweetheart?"

"I am, Evan. I am. I was so scared."

Evan sat up, gathering her close, not mindful of the others in the room.

"I'm okay. You're okay, aren't you?" He felt her nod against his cheek. "Praise God that you are. He has protected us and brought you home again, sweetheart."

———

"I finally get that, Evan." She leaned back to look up at him, seeing that look in his eyes that said she was so special and his. "We need to heal, but He is the Great Physician."

"That He is. All we have to do is reach to touch the hem of His garment, sweetheart." Evan shifted to watch the others. "Everyone's okay? Everett?"

Everett grimaced as he rubbed at the back of his head. "I'm fine, Evan. They got the drop on me and shouldn't have."

Evan grinned. "You tried hard to put up a fight. That's why." He frowned as he looked around. "It's over, isn't it?"

Joe nodded. "It is, Evan. Between the three of you young people, you have brought down an illegal empire that started so many years ago. We'll talk more, but right now, let's spend time in prayer."

Chapter 49

Two weeks later, Dooley approached Flannery and Evan as they stood at the lakeshore, staring across at Elm Island. He had had word from the jail where the Waters brothers had been transferred to and he needed to speak with them.

"Dooley? You're here?" Flannery reached to hug him.

"I am. And how are you this fine day?" He grinned at her as she frowned at him. "Wipe the frown, Flannery. You have your life back."

"I know." She sounded disgruntled for a moment. "Did we ever get an explanation for that baby's blanket?"

"We did. The Earl sent it, hoping to spook you into leaving. That didn't work. We understand from the information provided to us by an undercover officer that they were behind everything you two went through. They were the ones who attempted to kidnap you when Evan stepped in."

"I still don't get what they wanted."

"You. You were a threat to them, they thought. Someone set you up, Flannery. That was someone that you trusted years ago." He watched with compassion as she thought through the people she knew. "Your old physician, Flannery. He was in on their drug dealing."

"Him? All those years ago? I don't understand."

"He told them that you had found out what they were up to, had seen them kill someone and that you would go to the authorities with that information. They tracked you all this time, with you staying just ahead of them. He has been arrested."

"Okay. Good, I think. I mean, I really didn't know him that well. I was only his patient for a few months before I moved on." Flannery leaned back against Evan, his arms around her.

Evan finally spoke. "You're here for another reason, Dooley."

"I am. The Duke and the Earl managed to get into a brawl with other prisoners. The Duke was killed. The Earl is in the prison hospital ward. They don't expect him to survive."

"Justice." Flannery's voice was a mere whisper. "Vengeance is mine, sayeth the Lord. I will repay." She leaned back to look up at Evan. "We talked about that just a bit ago."

"And He has avenged you."

"The body in the garden?" Flannery shared a look with Evan.

"The Duke did that as a threat and warning to you, Flannery. That you could expect the same unless you cooperated with him. The hit on you, Evan? That was the Earl. It was the Earl's men who attacked you after you freed yourself from the cabin and then dumped you two on that trail, never expecting you to be found again."130

Dooley stayed for a while longer before he walked away, praise in his heart that his friends were safe and that they no longer had to fear, a prayer for them as they determined just where it was they were heading. He thought a wedding was in order, but he wasn't even sure about that. He knew Lydia had returned to the big city, just to finish off what she had started and that she had plans to return to their town, to set up a counselling service for those in need. Lydia had found the niche that needed her.

———

Epilogue

Evan watched as Flannery moved towards him as she walked the path between his cabin and where she called home at present. He knew that she wouldn't be there long, not if he had anything to say about it and he was sure he did.

Flannery's face lit up as she saw him waiting, arms open to hug her close to him. She felt content, that she had found what she had been searching for. What had she been searching for? Love and a home.

"Doing okay?" Evan's voice whispered in her ear. It had been two months since their adventure, as they called it, ended.

"I am, finally." She looked up at him, seeing the look in his eyes.

"Come on, sweetheart. I have something for you." Evan reached for her hand, leading her to the deck and the chairs that she had insisted needed to be there.

Seating her, he knelt beside her, causing her to frown at him.

"Flannery, when I stopped to help you that day, I didn't know that I would find such a wonderful, caring, compassionate woman who loves my God so much. When you disappeared, I thought my world had come to an end." He reached for her hand, a ring appearing in his.

Flannery drew in her breath. She was loved, she now knew and by the man God had planned just for her.

"Will you marry me, be my helpmeet, walk through life at my side, serving God with me? I love you dearly, sweetheart."

Flannery could only nod, her voice choked with tears as she whispered that she loved him too. Evan reached to gather her close to him, a kiss on her lips as they sealed their love.

A while later, Flannery looked up, seeing the sunset on the lake and knowing that would be the view she would live with for as long as they lived here. She prayed that it would be a long time.

"Evan? Have you had any word from Dooley?"

"I have. The men have taken plea deals. We don't have to testify. It is over, sweetheart. Our adventure that almost killed us, separated us for what seemed so long, is over." He grinned at her. "And now I have to decide what I want to do."

"And that would be?" Flannery waited, knowing that he would tell her when he was ready.

"I have had so many opportunities come in. The Waters place? It was offered to me after it was confiscated by the town. I plan to set up it up as a retreat for people in transition. Everett will come in and work with us. He has been looking for something. It will specifically be targeted to those who are victims of crime. Abe has been around. He has put me in contact with a friend of his, a retired forensics psychologist who has offered to help. God has led here, sweetheart."

"I am so glad, Evan. It is what we need to do. I know I could have used something like that."

"I know." Evan sat back after lifting Flannery to his knee and just cuddled with his sweetheart, gladness in his heart. He began to pray, to praise God for His protection, His leading and for His blessing on their plans.

The two finally just sat, content for the moment to be together, knowing that their engagement would be short, Flannery insisting on that, and then they would walk, hand in hand, in service of their God.

Dear Readers:

Thank you for taking the time to read the story of Evan and his lady, Flannery. I have no idea where her name came from. Back to my Irish roots on my mother's side, I suspect. Her dreams? They did come true. His dream? I imagine they did as well.

What dream have you been holding on to, not yet fulfilled? God is there. He delights in our dreams, our wishes. My dream, that only my mother knew about, was to write a novel. *The Sparrow* was written in 2017, dedicated to her, seven years after she passed away. She had faith in my dream, just asking me why didn't I? That is a dream I had had since a child. Did God allow me to fulfill? You bet He did. My only prayer with my books is that they reach someone and direct to a stronger walk with him.

I have fun with my characters. Well-loved ones walk back and forth between novels. Abe, Emma, and his security team have done that so many times. I miss this group of men and ladies, all of whom had what they term as adventures. I never know which book they will walk into. That's the fun of having unruly characters that take over the plot line. Their stories are in the *His Guardians* series.

And just where did Evan appear from? He was an undercover officer in *The Chain of Life*, where he did work to help take down a man named Blackmore.

Give God your dreams. It may take a while to see them fulfilled. Some won't be, but He chooses the ones that are just right for us and in His timing. Trust Him with those.

May God bless each one of you. May you find His hand covering you and protecting you in whatever it is that you face.

Ronna